I0730994

A MATTER OF JUSTICE

5 ORIGINAL SMALL TOWN SHORT STORIES
FIGHTING FOR JUSTICE

J. A. BOUMA

EmmausWay
P R E S S

INTRODUCTION

A few years ago, I'd been kicking around the idea of creating a fictional smallish town in West Michigan for several months, thinking it could be a fun way to tell the stories of people living life while exploring faith, taking a page out of Stephen King's playbook with Castle Rock, Maine, and John Grisham's Clanton, Mississippi.

Then the Great Pandemic of 2020 hit, and it seemed like the perfect time to kick off the project! After all, I was stuck inside like most people with lots of time on my hands. Figured I should keep busy, because as they say: idle hands are the devil's tools! Sounded like great fun anyway, spending my newfound time with a new set of characters in a new world outside my normal world that had been blown up by a crazy virus, but also something different from the usual story world of my existing fiction.

Thus was born Mill Creek Junction, as well as a host of characters who show up in the Christmas-themed collection of original short stories set in the small Midwest town.

Like all towns, big or small, bad things happen to good

people. Quite often, those bad things are thanks to bad people; scoundrels abound in any size town. And it takes a special cast of characters to right the wrongs, especially in small towns where the shadows seem to grow darker, grow sideways for any number of reasons. Whether because of punishing poverty or depleting government coffers, those who fight for justice are a rare, special breed.

And this collection of five original short stories celebrates them, sharing their stories and singing their praises.

It's an ode to small-town heroes who wonder to themselves *Where's the justice?*, and then do something about it. From unsung police chiefs trying their darnedest to serve and protect; to small-town lawyers trying to get by and needing a reminder why they do the things they do; and even assistant prosecuting attorneys caught up in small-town politics—Gerald Roller, Gideon O'Donnell, and Annabelle Kirkland remind us that justice, in all its forms, is something to fight for.

This theme of justice is a deeply biblical one. It's something God cares about; it is close to his very own heartbeat. Which is why he calls on us to seek it, to fight for it, to go to the mat to see it flow in our own towns.

Martin Luther King Jr. quoted one of these verses from the Good Book, Amos 5:24, his most oft quoted portion from the Bible: *'But let justice roll down like waters, and righteous ness like an ever-flowing stream.'* His vision was like Gideon's, Annabelle's, and Chief Rollers: He longed for justice to flow freely through America's streets, precisely because he understood the Creator, the Lord Almighty, declared such a thing good, right, and worth fighting for.

For as the prophet Micah reminds us, *'He has told you, O mortal, what is good; and what does the Lord require of you but to do justice, and to love kindness, and to walk humbly with your God?'*

May we follow in their footsteps, realizing that all of life is a matter of justice, for this is what the Lord requires of us.

Grace and peace,
~J.A. Bouma • February 2022

STORY 1

SERVE AND PROTECT

WHAT A CRAPPY DAY *this is gonna be.*

It was raining cats and dogs. Cliché, I know, but it was all I got after a week with the town back in full swing without so much as a jaywalking citation to hand out!

And it was, too—a wicked storm gusting in off Lake Michigan and barreling full-force down Main Street. If I could give it a ticket for reckless endangerment, I would. But, alas, Mill Creek Junction doesn't pay me to ticket midsummer storms. Only hot-rodding teenagers driving ten years too early, if you ask me, and red-light running grannies driving twenty years too late, if you ask me twice.

But what do I know? I'm just the Junction's police chief. Don't make the rules, just enforce 'em. Me and my nine underlings. Serve and protect, that's what we do.

I took a sip of my coffee and grimaced, but then snorted a chuckle. "Red-light running grannies is right, God love 'em." And I did. Had me one of my own, a cantankerous little, bitty grandma who taught me a thing or twenty-two with the backside of her hand.

Speaking of which, should probably stop by later today,

see how she's doing after the scare her nursing home had the past few months with COVID-19.

But first things first.

It was a new day of a new week and I was itchin' to get back in the saddle and solve some real crimes, help some folks in imminent danger. Instead, I was pulling up to Millie's on Main as Noah's Ark floated by—I snorted another laugh at the thought of that fairytale coming to life, sort of like another one of our clichés, 'When pigs fly!'—readying to cart the Rev around all morning on some community policing gig thrown at me last minute by Mayor Goodall.

I scoffed, making the turn off Straight Street (which ironically ran parallel to Gay Street, hand to the Universe!) and gunning it for destiny in a huff that would normally get a big fat ticket. But since I was the Big Cheese, that wasn't happenin' anytime soon!

Stewed some more as I neared the diner. How could the mayor stick me with babysitting the town Baptist preacher? Knew I shouldn't have skipped my Tai Chi lesson this morning. But Buster needed those gnarly nails of his trimmed, and Tilly needed a good shampoo, and Rex was near out of medicine, and Salmon was coughing up more than furballs. So off to PetLand I went to cut the one dog's nails, and get the cat its bath, and then get a refill for dog number two, all before cat numero dos got to the vet for a checkeroo.

Nobody wants a whino on their hands, I know. And since I was a recovering alcoholic, my kind of wine was the whine kind. So I pulled the horse to the curb, the brakes squeaking something fierce, put her in park, then closed my eyes and took a breath.

In the words of the Big G Costanza: Serenity now...

I put the horse to sleep and climbed out, grabbing my trusty brown leather trooper fedora that had been with me since graduating the academy. I hiked up my pants, sizing up my stomping grounds with a satisfied glance before heading inside.

Place smelled as it always did on Monday mornings: Like a million freakin' dollars, of bacon and cheesy eggs and onions, pancakes and waffles. The black and white tile floors with off-white walls and booths done up in light pink and blue were practically dripping with it, which suited me fine.

"Mornin', Chief Roller," Patty said from behind the counter, a middle-aged woman with heft in all the right places.

I took my hat off and flashed her my pearly whites. "Mornin' yourself, Peppermint Patty."

Leaning over the counter, she giggled and threw me a wry grin. "Flirting before, eight? How totally unlike you..."

"Only for you, dear. Say, is the Rev in yet?" I spun back toward the room filled to the brim, throwing the social distancing guidelines right out the window. Could bust every one of 'em for it, too. Maybe I'll round 'em all up before I leave. Wouldn't that be a nice get on my quota sheet!

She pointed in the corner. "In the back. Finishing up a plate of scrambled eggs and toast. You joining him?"

"More like he's joining me. Thanks, Patty. Have yourself a good one."

I'd eaten before coming, a bowl of Wheaties to get the gut back into a more appropriate size. So I lifted the glass topper to the platter of gooey goodness that was the Death Star to my sugar inhibitions, pulling me in with rainbow sprinkles and chocolate and cream. A man's gotta give in to at least one vice. Alcohol about did me in, so it was donuts 'til the grave.

Grabbing a chocolate-glazed doughnut, I threw a fiver on the counter and told Patty to keep the change.

Breakfast of champions, right there.

I took a bite, my mouth filling with a surprise cream filling, and sauntered over to the Rev, offering a few howdy-dos to the citizens of the Junction along the way.

There he was, reading a book. No, a Bible. Figured. A preacher and a plate of eggs and a Bible. Apparently, my day was going to be filled with clichés.

"I see you're readying yourself for the ride, Rev. But no need to worry. Shouldn't get anywhere near Saint Pete's pearly gates today."

The man, Reiner Alden, turned around and offered a chuckle, a silver comb-over flapping in the breeze of his laughter and a spot of cheesy eggs staining his sweater vest.

"You got a little shmuts on the sweater vest, my friend."

"Oh, dear me!" He wiped it with his napkin, but only made it worse.

"Well, lookie thar," I voice called from behind. "A cop eating a donut. Go figure."

I turned around and frowned. Max Blade.

"Howdy, Chief Roller."

"Better watch yourself, Max."

"Or else what?" he said, folding his arms and giving me an eye I didn't like. "I'll find myself on the wrong side of one of your overused clichés?"

The Rev snorted a chuckle before taking a drink of coffee, working his napkin against the stain without success.

I felt the back of my neck redden from the insult. That Max Blade was gonna be the death of me!

Instead of giving the man all the fuel he needed to blow

more smoke, I turned back to the Rev. "You ready to get to it, Reverend?"

He stood. "That I am."

"Get to what?" said Max.

"Riding shotgun with the chief today. Does that mean I get to carry said shotgun?"

"In a word, no," I said. "There will be no shotgun toting. Only shotgun riding. Are you ready?"

He grinned. "Ready when you are!"

A bit too eager like for the day ahead. Just you wait buddy. Just you wait.

We said adios to Max and Patty and a few other patrons, then saddled up for the day.

First call of the morning came in as soon as we got into the car. A possible B&E.

"How exciting!" The Rev said, clapping his hands together.

"That's one way of putting it. Hold on tight, Rev."

I threw up the strobes and siren, then threw the horse into *Drive*, peeling out with a mean spin, tires squealing on the rain-slicked pavement. Turned out, all the drama wasn't necessary, as the site of the alleged criminal activity was just a few blocks up the road, at Nugent Barbershop.

Which struck me as an odd joint to break and enter into. Not much there but aftershave and scissors. Suppose the perp might need to give himself a shave and cut. Polish up a bit for a hot date. Though the prospects on that front had to be bleak if he was robbing a barbershop.

Yet there the dude was—or dudette, I suppose. I'm certainly an egalitarian when it comes to knucklehead criminals, though my experience with this level of knucklehead is they come from Mars instead of Venus.

But there he was, huddled up at the front entry in a

black overcoat, hat pulled up overhead, the dude wielding a hacksaw, ready to do a number on the doorknob and, indeed, break and enter into the joint.

Which also seemed odd. Why go through the front in the broad daylight morning when the back door was a better option?

We came up hot and heave, blaring and screeching to a halt.

Scaring the living crap-lights out of the perp!

I jumped out of the car and withdrew my trusty friend named Glock. God only knew what he might try with the hacksaw.

"Hold it right there, mist—"

The sight before me interrupted my own command.

The black hood had flapped back, revealing Old Man Nugent's shiny eight-ball head. Something I always found rather ironic. A bald barber? But what did I know.

I stuck my pistol in my holster with a huff.

"Fred!" I exclaimed with an edge of complaint to my voice. "What on earth are you doing?"

"What am I doing?" he exclaimed, waving around that hacksaw in a way that made me regret putting away my Glock. "What the hell are you doing, coming up on me like that?"

I put out my hands and took a few steps around the hood. "Got a call on a possible breaking and entering, that's why."

"Breaking and entering? But why, I own the joint!"

"You do look suspicious, Fred," the Rev said from the front seat, window rolled in a completely unhelpful manner.

Old Man Nugent squinted toward the passenger's side window. "Reverend Alden, is that you?"

"The man joined me for a little community policing effort today," I interjected, "but let's bring this back around to what on earth you're doing taking a hacksaw to your front door."

He looked at it and huffed. "Locked my keys inside, that's what."

"That's a bummer. But what about your backdoor? Would have avoided this whole misunderstanding I'm sure, seen as how some civilians saw you out front taking a hacksaw to your door!"

"Couldn't. That numbskull Max Blade parked a delivery truck clear in front of it, blocking the way! I should have you go arrest him for obstruction."

"Just say the word..." I muttered before reaching back inside the cruiser for a doohickey that should get the job done.

Retrieving the thing, I sauntered over to the lock and thrust it inside.

"What's that?" he asked.

"A little sidearm I like to keep handy for the mornings old men lock themselves out of their barbershops."

With a few twists, the door unlocked with a *click*, and the smell of Lysol and aftershave was wafting outside.

Old Man Nugent grabbed my hand and shook it. "Thanks, chief! Saved me a lot of headache busting through that there door knob. Next cut's on the house!"

"Don't mention."

After writing up a report, the paperwork never ceasing to amaze me even as long as I've been working the streets, we headed back out into the Junction for a little serve-and-protect drive.

Which yielded a big nothingburger.

Nada, zip, zilch! It was as if we were still on lockdown, Mill Creek was so quiet.

The Rev hummed to a top-40s pop station I'd rather do without. Straight oldies-but-goodies for me.

Nearing noon, I gave up the chase and we grabbed a bite to go from Subway at the Shell gas station on the edge of town. Figured a Cold Cut Combo with potato chips would do the body good after the chocolate doughnut.

Except the pimply faced sandwich chef screwed up, only putting up three of the four meats, forgetting the bologna, the best part. Had to go back for a redo, which set us back getting back out into the Junction. How one screws up a Cold Cut Combo is beyond me. Dude probably stashed the bologna for a midnight snack. Fifteen minutes later, finally got back in the saddle.

Then it happened.

In fact, I should probably thank the pimply faced sandwich chef for the screw up, because we probably would have been clear back into town by now. And we would have missed the ride of our lives.

A speeder, flying out of downtown at near sixty!

At minimum, the dude—or, again, dudette—was losing their license. If we were lucky, it was even a bigger kahuna than a flimsy speeding ticket!

Heart starting to rev up to full throttle, I yanked the radio and called it in. "Dispatch, we've got a 10-38 coming west of Main. A sixty in a twenty-five and possible GTA, stand by."

"Now this is nuts," the Rev said with a nervous giggle.

Throwing on the strobes and siren again, I agreed. Then pealed after perp numero dos, coming up hot and heavy to the bumper. A minivan, which was a bit unusual for such a crime. But desperate times called for desperate measures, I figured. Even nabbing grocery getters off suburban Karens with too much time on their hands.

Odd thing was, the car slowed, but kept right on going, beelining it for the Junction's border.

I blared the sirens, goosing it a little to make a warbling warning to let 'em know who was in charge.

That seemed to do the job.

The van screeched to a halt along the side of the road, dirt and dust blooming with perturbation. Love that word. Just rolls of the tongue. Just like the door.

Which just rolled right open!

Sending me scrambling out the door myself.

"Chief, where do you want—"

"Stay in the car!" I yelled, shoving a leg out on the pavement. The Rev did as he was told.

Stepping outside and whipping out my Glock, I shouted, "Stay in the car! Stay in the—"

And out stepped Ken Robertson.

Which made about as much sense as a one-legged mule!

"Ken?"

He put his arms out and stuttered, "Chief, you gotta help us! Barbara's in labor!"

"Labor?" I exclaimed, shoving my piece back in its holster and rushing to the man, ironically a blond-haired musclehead who looked like he just stepped off a toy catalogue.

He brought me around to the side, then slid open the door.

I gasped.

There she was, sprawled out on the back, soaked blanket underneath and breathing the Lamaze like it was nobody's business!

"Uh, uh," I stammered, brain spinning with uncertainty. Never encountered one of these before. "Should I call an ambulance?"

"Not necessary. We're close, but not that—"

A scream pierced the mid-afternoon like a sonic boom.

Apparently, they were closer than they thought.

"Just get us to Mercy General, chief! Already called ahead and they're ready for us. Can you escort us, part the traffic?"

"Like Moses at the Red Sea! Hop in."

I shuffled back to the squad car and leapt inside. I radioed dispatch about the false alarm, explaining we had a live-wire birth on our hands and was escorting them to Mercy.

"Was that Ken I saw?" the Rev asked, face fallen with concern. "I pray Barbara is alright? Is she OK?"

"Labor."

"What was that, Gerald?"

"Labor!" I replied. "She's having their baby."

"In the back seat of the van?"

I flared the strobes and sirens back up and peeled out in front of the Robertson's van, then got to work.

"Not if I can help it..."

Racing down the state highway, we soon reached the hospital built a decade ago with private dollars and few federal ones thrown in for good measure. Wasn't nearly as good as the two in downtown Grand Rapids, but they got the job done.

And apparently delivered babies at the drop of a...well, baby!

Pulling up to the emergency doors, the poor kid was already crowning. I had called ahead through dispatch and a doc was standing by. Had to climb into the back of the van and deliver him then and there.

By all the goodness left in the Universe, the kid came out quick and easy. Tried to get 'em to name him Jerry, but it was no use. Henry it was, which was one of those ironic Millennial names, I guess, about two generations too late. Will probably scar the kid for life, too, but whatever

The Rev said a prayer with the couple and off we went.

By that time, I was ready to call it a day coming up with bupkis on the serve and protect end of things.

"How about we call it day, Rev?"

"Whatever you think, chief," he said. "You're the boss."

"I think it's time to roll. I'll bring you home, if it's alright with you."

He agreed, and we headed back to his place.

Leaving Mercy General, we trudged back down the state highway and back to Main Street running through the Junction. Turning onto Cherry Lane off Main, the Rev gave a holler.

"Looks like someone needs help!"

He was pointing down the road at a little kid waving his arms all frantic and helpless, like he needed us to stop. Looked like the Clawson boy, Jason, eight or nine.

Was his mom or dad in trouble, or their house on fire, or some perp trying to swipe little kiddies from Mill Creek streets?

Throwing on the strobes and siren, I gunned the horse and brought it up to the kid.

"Chief Wolla, Chief Wolla!" Jason said, his Rs not fully formed, reminding him of the priest from *The Princess Bride*.

"What's happened, son? You al—"

"Come quick, come quick! You just gotta help!"

Not able to get a word in edge-wise before the kid took off for home, I jumped off the horse after him.

He led me to a large oak anchored out front of a two-story brown bricker, a nice thing bought with bank money, Jack Clawson being in the financial industry or some boujee gig. Then he pointed, the tree towering above us.

"It's Patches, Chief Wolla!"

I didn't understand. "Patches?" I said, a hand planted at my hips and another shielding my eyes from the sun.

"My vewy, vewy favwit cat."

A looked at the kid, face twisted up with confusion,

"He's stuck up in the bwanches," he hollered, pointing back at the tree.

A cat? My life has been reduced to animal control?

But, being a cat guy myself, I understood. And, being an eight-year-old boy with a vewy, vewy favwit cat at one time, I also understood.

So I nodded and patted the kid on the head. "Stand back, Jason, and let me work my magic."

I saddled up to the massive trunk, rolled up my sleeves, grabbed a massive bough, gave a good heave-ho, and started climbing.

Couldn't see the thing at first with the mess of leaves popping through, black with patches of white, apparently. How original. But eventually I spotted it, way up there, probably thirty feet up.

Reaching it, I said, "Here, kitty, kitty, kitty."

He hissed at me, throwing up a paw and baring its teeth and raising its fur something fierce.

Ungrateful little furball!

But I played nice, throwing up a smile and taking out from my front pocket a piece of leftover potato chips I'd saved for later.

"Here, kitty, kitty, kitty."

That seemed to do the trick. He padded forward,

raising his nose with a sniff and wiggling his whiskered nose with curiosity.

Then he took a bit, and another. I grabbed him around the back, stuffing him at my chest as he kept at the chip, then started for home.

Reaching the bottom, I leaped to the ground, the furball leaping from arms and into Jason's.

Have to admit, Jason's wide grin, tears streaking down his face at the reunion, did my heart right seeing him so happy to have his pet back.

"Chief Wolla, Chief Wolla, you're my vewy, vewy favwit police chief!"

I couldn't help but smile—at the compliment as much as the accent.

I mussed up Jason's hair. "Don't mention it, kid. Now take good care of him, alright?"

"I will!"

I saddled back up on the horse, recounting the story to the Rev, then we drove the guy home.

The drive back was a silent one. Mostly because I was stewing at not seeing any action. Had been that way for months, and it made me second guess my chosen career path. I'd signed up to serve and protect. Scoping out the bad guys, creeping up on the knuckleheads, busting down the doors, and kicking ass and taking names.

Not helping old men into their barbershops, and people get their babies delivered, and definitely not fishing cats out of trees!

I bit at my lower lip as we drove on, feeling like it had been a royal waste of a day. Alright, so I birthed a baby and saved a cat. That's what doctors and animal control was for. Not Mill Creek's finest. Not me.

Serve and protect, that was my job. And it had been a long time since I'd seen hide or tail of those ones.

We pulled up to the Reverend's parish house sitting next to Mill Creek Baptist Church. A modest one-level white eyesore with black shutters, a pair of those little boy and girl statues sitting next to a fake wooden well in a garden butting up to a sidewalk leading to a sagging front porch, those wretched dandelions scattered about and shedding their white seeds like leprosy.

Screamed cliché, which was about the way life went nowadays.

I drove up his short driveway and walked the man to his front door. The Rev insisted it wasn't necessary, but I worried he'd keel over with how old he was. A wicked crack ran across the poor thing. Apparently, a preacher's salary doesn't leave room for a bag of cement! And weeds jutted up this way and that. Apparently neither does it pay for a sack of weed n' feed!

Reaching the porch, he said, "Thanks for letting me come along today, chief. What a day!"

"Sorry it couldn't have been more...entertaining. A bit of a letdown, really."

He twisted up his face as if confused. "A letdown? Are you kidding me? What a thrill it was!"

I laughed nervously, not understanding his meaning. "Thrill? Far from it, Rev."

"But it was. Look at all we did." Then he corrected himself: "What *you* did."

"But I didn't do anything!"

"What are you talking about? You did plenty today."

"So I saved a cat. Big whoop."

"And delivered a baby! Not to mention helping an old man get back into his business."

"Yeah, yeah. But far from anything in the ol' job description."

"What did you expect? To solve an open serial killer case from years back?"

I drew in a breath and folded my arms, intending not to huff but doing just that. The man had a point.

The Rev gestured toward the porch steps and he took a seat. I hesitated, wondering what the man was up to. Last thing I needed was an earful of Baptist sermonizing! But I relented, joining him at the top.

"Let me give you a bit of advice, Gerald," he said, leaning against a wooden support I feared would give way. "Something a minster mentor said to me awhile back."

I rolled my eyes. *Here we go...*

"He says to me, 'Tommy'—I was Tommy back in the day, before my head turned silver!"

I smiled. "I bet."

"'Tommy,' he says, 'you strut around here, going from this meeting to that meeting, trying to make a difference, trying to save people from ruin. And that's all well and good. But the good Lord above neither wants nor needs any of it.'"

I leaned back against another questionable wooden support, crossing my arms. "Really? He said that?"

He nodded. "Sure did. He says to me, 'What the Lord wants instead is two things.'"

Our money and our manhood? Right?

Didn't say it, but I sure thought it. Had been about the extent of my experience with the Church.

Instead, I said: "What's that, Rev?"

He leaned in with a twinkle in his eyes, one end of his mouth curling upward in a way that made me slightly uncomfortable. He said, "Availability and faithfulness."

"Availability and faithfulness?" I think I turned up my brow at the words. Probably seemed snooty, but it was more that it made not a lick of sense.

The Rev nodded. "That's right. All God wants from us is to be available and faithful. To him and his calling on our lives. And by where I was sitting, you did that today. You were available to the needs of the Junction. And you were faithful in your execution of your very, very important role as community leader in helping the good people of Mill Creek. Serve and protect, isn't that right?"

I didn't know whether to laugh or cry, the Rev touched me so. I nodded instead. "That's right. Serve and protect."

He slapped a hand on my knee and offered a chuckle. "That you did, Gerald. That you did! You helped a woman bring her baby into the world. And you helped a young boy rescue his stranded cat. Not sure how much better you can get at serving and protecting."

I smiled to myself. Man did have a point.

"And now you can add another two to the lineup," he said.

I smiled at the Rev now. "Available and faithful?"

He nodded. "Available and faithful."

How about that...

I smirked and said, "You know, Reverend, I do believe that was the first sermon of yours I've ever had the pleasure of setting my ears to."

The Rev laughed. "Well, if you thought that was preaching, you should come by some Sunday!"

I bet!

"You know what, Rev? You're all right."

He laughed again. "Good to know. You are too, chief. And if you ever need another man to ride shotgun, you know where to find me!"

"That I do Rev."

We said our goodbyes, and I got back into my car. I threw the horse into 'Drive' and pulled back out onto Main Street. The clouds had pulled back some, revealing a sunny blue and a world freshly watered. I considered the day, the newborn, the saved cat.

Serve and protect is right.

Then I considered the Rev's words.

Available and faithful.

A smile crept across my face.

Not a bad day after all.

A MATTER OF JUSTICE

"I'LL TAKE a grande extra-hot flat white with sugar-free vanilla, please."

I slung my purse up on the counter and started rifling through it for my Starbucks card. I knew it was in there somewhere. But between the mascara, lipstick, eyeliner, deodorant, and extra pantyhose—because Lord knows a girl has got to keep an extra pair just in case!—I wasn't having any luck.

"Oh, and would you be a good dear and add an extra shot?"

"One of those days, Annabelle?" Trisha said, leaning over the counter and eyeing my oversized purse that serviced as an office away from office.

I sighed, pushing a stubborn lock of strawberry blonde hair my mama gave me back into place. "That it is. If only I could find my card..."

"Don't worry about it, sister. It's on the house this morning."

I looked up, frowning with no small amount of embarrassment. "Really? Are you sure? I mean, I can come back later once I find the darn thing..." I went back to the purse, rummaging through it with about the same amount of luck.

"Seriously, sister. Not a problem. Doubt Howard Shults is going to miss the fiver."

I smiled and clutched my chest. "Bless your heart, Trish. I owe you one."

"Next time Chief Roller gives me a speeding ticket, I'll come knocking."

"Deal!" I tossed her a buck and slid to the end of the bar to wait for my drink.

A rumble of thunder shuddered through the place of exposed wood and brick. It was a quaint little thing that bespoke its Midwest roots stretching back to the founding of Mill Creek Junction back in the late 1800s. And actually, it used to be one of my fav coffee shops, a little, bitty thing owned by Mayor Goodall's wife, Millie, as a second cash stream aside from her diner. Not sure what happened, but they had to close and that darn Siren came swooping in to capitalize on the coffee traffic, another piece of Small Town, America, losing its soul along the way. I'm a sucker for Starbucks like the next girl, but Corporate America really sucks sometimes.

"Howdy, Cameron," I said to the college kid with gauges the size of nickels manning the espresso machine, a crown of blond hair stuffed under a navy stocking cap. He had that boy-next-door look about him but was trying to pull a bad-boy look that looked like fake news.

The kid looked up and brightened. "Hey, Annabelle! Or, should I say, good morning, Assistant Prosecuting Attorney Kirkland," he added with a bow.

I giggled. "Oh, stop that. How many times have I told you that you make me sound old? Annabelle is fine."

He chuckled and held up his hands in surrender. "Then

Annabelle it is. Thought I saw your flat white come through." He held up my cup and winked, flashing me those perfect white teeth with that perfect dimple that threw off the whole bad-boy gig.

I flashed him a smile and winked back, throwing up my hands. "Guilty as charged!"

What, can't a late-thirty-year-old woman flirt with a small-town college kid?

Then I had a depressing thought: Had I married my high school sweetheart like I had planned before he left me at the altar, literally, I very well could have been old enough to be Cameron's mother. The smile quickly faded, and I lost my appetite for the flat white.

We shared a laugh and the shrill of my phone gave me an excuse to exit stage left, pronto. I fished it out of my purse, finding my Starbucks card along the way, and glanced at its face.

Dean Lawlor. The Junction's chief Prosecuting Attorney.

I sighed. The boss calling before eight was never a good sign. And the fact I'd just been flirting with his son made it doubly bad.

Grabbing my finished drink from the counter, I tossed Cameron my other buck and nodded goodbye as I jostled the phone against my head.

"Mornin', boss. Little early for a ring-a-ding-ding, isn't it? Hope all is well at—"

"Have you gotten a call yet from O'Donnell?" Dean said with an interruptive rush.

"Gideon?" I said, cursing myself for getting too casual with the other side of the aisle. He and I were friendly enough outside of our adversarial process at the courthouse, but Dean hated his guts. Probably because Gideon was good at what he did.

I heard him clear his throat on the other end, as if swallowing back a shot of vinegar at my mention of his name. He said, "That would be the one. Anyway, he's going to come to you sometime today about the Pentwell case and try to make a deal."

"Pentwell case?" I asked, setting my drink on an annoyingly tiny table in front of a picture window, and squeezing into a seat with my back to the door. "Isn't that the simple possession case, the one with Trevor Pentwell?"

Dean laughed. "Nothing's ever simple, you know that! Especially when one of the city counsel member's son is involved."

I sighed with understanding, popping the top and slurping some foam off. It was laced with dark espresso, the earthy, smoky notes tingling my tastebuds and taking me away for the slightest moment.

"Annabelle, you there?" Dean asked.

"Sorry. But I don't understand. I was planning to kick the thing because it involved Claudia's son. Not that I'm interested in kickbacks or anything, but it was a few joints, anyway. Nothing big."

He snorted a laugh. "A few joints? Are you kidding me?"

"Like, three or four, if I recall."

"Try three or four *ounces!*"

I took another sip of my flat white, growing increasingly disinterested and irritated. "How much is that? I thought a joint held an ounce of weed."

"Try a *gram* of weed per joint!"

"*Per joint?* That's a lot of weed!" I said, a little too loud for comfort.

I glanced over at the bar, Cameron giving me a nod while Trish and another customer I didn't recognize looked over with disgust, or concern, or both.

"Yeah, try two shopping bags full," Dean said, bringing me back to the convo that was growing weird.

"I don't understand what the problem is. Michigan legalized marijuana for personal use. I don't see this as a big deal, Dean."

"No, see, that's where you're wrong. The mayor has other plans."

I shifted in my chair and took a mouthful of espresso-laced milk this time. "The mayor has other plans? What the heck does that mean?"

"Look. There's been some trouble, apparently, and with elections coming up, the mayor would like a reshuffle on the counsel. Figured the mother of a convicted pothead wouldn't stand a chance against someone else he had in mind who was a bit more...amenable. Anyway, as you know, our office is staffed by appointment. Not me, of course, as an elected judicial representative. And the way the Mill Creek Junction charter was written way back in the olden days of yore, that appointment comes by the chief executive."

Now I needed a shot of Bailey's, because I got where he was going with this one.

Mayor Goodall was that chief executive of Mill Creek Junction.

"What are you saying, Dean, exactly? And please spell it out for me, just so I'm clear on my marching orders. From the chief executive."

"Now, Annabelle, I'm not giving you marching orders, per se."

"You just indicated spiking the Pentwell case would be politically problematic."

"Just use your discretion, alright? Marijuana is a big deal. A gateway drug, you know. And who knows? He may even be dealing in larger quantities. Which means this is a matter of law."

"Good Lord, Dean! It wasn't a U-Haul full, it was clearly for personal use. And now we're making a simple possession case into intent to distribute?"

"I'm just saying, use your discretion. But illegal intent sounds about right. Again, it's a matter of law. Gotta go. Catch you later, and give me an update if you hear from O'Donnell."

The call ended, and I tossed the phone back in my purse.

"Oh, I'll give you something, you sorry sonofa—"

I was interrupted by the jangle of the bell above the door behind me, a rushing breeze from the early morning storm throwing its sweat against my backside.

I gave a start and turned around on habit.

My face fell, and it got splashed with another dose of storm sweat before the blasted door closed back tight.

"Crapola..."

I spun back around in my chair, head down and face buried behind my flat white.

There he was. My nemesis. Come for his morning coffee or triple-shot, nonfat, extra-whip Caramel Macchiato or whatever frou-frou drink that was his poison. Hair all slicked from just the right amount of product keeping those wavy dark locks in place, a golf umbrella keeping it perfectly dry and coiffed. That dark blue suit pressed to perfection with the starch-white shirt and bright-red power tie that told the world I'm Mr. Somebody, I'm Mr. McDreamy, in all of my—

"Annabelle!" McDreamy said—or Gideon, rather.

I snapped my head up out from behind my flat white with a smile, eyes going wide and mouth dropping with feigned surprise.

"My land," I giggled, playing with my hair and getting my Southern belle on. "Gideon O'Donnell. As I live and breathe. Why, whatever are you doing here?"

He frowned and plopped down in the seat across from me. "Save the Southern pixie routine. You know I come here for morning coffee as much as I know you do. Can I sit and chat about something quick?"

Now I frowned. "You already did..."

He smiled. "Excellent!"

He picked up his drink at the end of the bar, presumably having ordered ahead of time with his app. Then he reached in his leather briefcase for what I presume was his Pentwell file.

"What are you drinking?"

He glanced at his cup. "Mint tea?"

"Tea? At Starbucks?"

He shrugged, still fishing. "Thought I'd switch it up."

"You, switch things up?"

He flashed me a grin. "All the time."

I rolled my eyes and leaned back, taking a sip of my flat white and staring outside as rain slapped the window something fierce as he continued to rummage. All I wanted with a smidge of peace and quiet before my day began. Maybe even get a jump on it was my frothed whole milk and caramel espresso blend. Yet here's McDreamy, readying to read me the RIOT Act on his pothead kid right after Dean pretty well made me a party to political cronyism!

"Nice hair, by the way," Gideon said, retrieving his file.

I raised a brow and cocked my head. "Nice hair?"

"Yeah. Are you doing something new with it?"

"Why is it whenever you need something from me you compliment my hair?"

"I was just—"

"Do you compliment Dean Lawlor's hair when you come begging for a deal?"

He laughed out loud, nearly choking on his tea. "Uh, no."

"Then why—"

"Look! I was just making conversation, alright? Goodness..." he mumbled before taking another sip of tea.

"Just treat me like one of the other fellas in my office, would you?"

He went to reply, then closed his mouth and nodded. Good lad.

I did sort of bite his head off, though. Wasn't my proudest moment, and I wasn't sure why I did it. But it was true. Never would a man compliment another dude's haircut. It's only us women who get that sort of treatment when they come calling, hat in hand.

Regardless, I shouldn't have bitten his head off.

So I held out my hands.

He furrowed his brow. "What's going on?"

"Here's your head back."

One end of his mouth curled upward. Then he took back his imaginary head and plopped it on his own like a hat.

"Where were we?" I asked, taking a sip of my latte that was now too warm for my liking. Piping hot was the only way to go in my book.

"The Pentwell case."

I looked off at the ceiling, as if I was trying to recall the details of that particular case among the myriad of cases my little APA brain was trying to manage at the moment.

"Oh, that's right," I feigned. "Possession, right?"

He nodded. "That's right—"

"With intent to distribute, wasn't it?"

He nearly choked again. "No! There was no intent to distribute and you know it. Are you adding that charge to the kid? No way you'd make that stick in court!"

"Relax, hot shot. Just messing with you."

He took a breath to respond, then closed his mouth again.

I brought out some files myself and started rifling through them. Again, feigning confusion about the case: "How much did he possess when he was pulled over?"

Gideon leaned forward and licked his lips. "Just under four ounces. Now, I know the legal limit is two and a half while driving, but the kid is clean. Blood came back negative for DUI. He's never been in trouble with the law. In fact, half of it wasn't even his. Just his friends. So separately, they fall well under the legal limit."

I nodded. "Uh, huh." I continued to rifle, taking sips here and there of my flat white gone the other side of lukewarm now.

"Then there's the probable cause issues, which I can almost guarantee I'll make stick, kicking the case anyway."

More uh-uhhing, more rifling, another sip.

"And since he's sixteen and this is his first offense, it's a $100 fine. Which makes this whole thing a big waste of time for you and me both. Because I don't know about you, but I charge way more than a hundred benjamins an hour!"

He laughed and flashed me those straight, white teeth and those turquoise eyes I must confess has caused me to stumble a time or two.

"So..."

"Huh?" I said with a start, mouth open and the realization dawning I'd been staring at McDreamy for who knew how long! I closed it and took a breath, pushing back that pesky lock that falls at the most inopportune time.

I cleared my throat and took another sip. "So, what?"

"So, how about you do me a solid—No," Gideon started over, putting up a finger, "do it for the kid. No need to waste our time or sully a fine, upstanding Eagle Scout with a record that resulted from a misunderstanding anyway."

I frowned. *Fine, upstanding Eagle Scout...*Give me a break McDreamy!

Instead, I said: "Here's what I'll do. I'll look over the file this afternoon and get back to you. See what I can pull—"

"This afternoon?" he said with interruption. "We've got the hearing in—" he checked his watch, a big, chunky, chrome thing that put an exclamation point on those benjamins he went on about. "Looks like two hours now."

"Two hours?" I checked my own wrist, sad at the Kohls special hanging limply. Then my neck started reddening at what Dean was putting me through, knowing Gideon would come calling at the eleventh hour and put me in a bind.

But, well...I liked my job, and frankly wanted to keep it. Despite the blowhard I worked for and the blowhard who appointed me.

So I put on my big girl pants and said, "Sorry. I can't do it. We're going to trial on this one."

His face fell. Hard. "What do you mean, you can't do it?"

"Well, it's 3.8 ounces while driving, piled in a bag, and Michigan law is clear."

"Wait a second!" He leaned forward and pointed that finger at me now. "It seemed like you didn't even know what I was talking about fifteen minutes ago, and now you're spouting off details of the case like you knew it by heart?"

Crapola...

I took a breath and offered a weak smile. "It's not like that. I—"

Gideon stood and snatched his tea from the table. Then he grabbed his briefcase and flashed me that grin of his I at once loathe and love. "See you in court."

I slumped back and took a drink of my flat white, grimacing at the cold milk and hating my morning.

Dean, I'm gonna kill you something fierce...

Two hours later, I was running up the stone court-house stairs, nearly slipping on the final one before lunging into the back end of an officer whose name slipped my mind.

We exchanged pleasantries, and I managed to make it through the metal detector without incident. Those things always seemed to have my number, fingering me for the most mundane of offenses. Stray rings or keys or coins. Not today, thank sweet Jesus! Because in one minute I would kick off a pre-trial hearing with tardiness, and that's the last thing I needed standing before—

I stopped in the middle of the hallway, my face scrunching up with dread.

"Crapola..." I double checked the docket, then checked it again to make sure I'd read it right.

Yep. I had. Judge Joey Heller it was.

Things kept getting worse. I should have stayed in bed.

No matter. I'd argue my pants off and take names along the way!

Finding a new confidence, I pushed through the double wood doors and strode down the aisle carpeted with a 70s special mustard weave just as the little man a hundred pounds soaking wet with those beady little eyes and haircut 80s-glam rock wanted back.

I giggled as I slid into the table at my side of the aisle. The haircut 80s-glam rock wanted—

"Something amusing, Ms. Kirkland?"

I snorted a laugh, more out of surprise than humor. Then quickly went stoic. "No, Your Majesty—I mean, Your Honor."

This day was turning sour right quick...

"Your Honor," Gideon said, standing up. "I think we can put this trial to rest here and now. I move for an immediate dismissal, with prejudice."

"Oh, come on!" I said. "You haven't even heard our case yet."

"I agree, counselor," Judge Heller said, leaning forward. "A little early for grandstanding for a dismissal. Even for you, Gideon."

I tried suppressing a grin, but struggled.

"So what say you, Ms. Kirkland?"

I took a breath and straightened. "As you can see from the affidavit proffered by the attending officer, Brett Vander-Woude pulled over Trevor Pentwell for failure to stop. Upon coming up to the driver's side door to attend to what he assumed was a simple traffic stop, the officer smelled the distinct odor of marijuana pouring out from the—"

"Pouring out?" Gideon interrupted. "A little dramatic, don't you think, Annabelle?"

I went to object but didn't have to.

"Counselor," the judge interjected, "ease up and let her finish. Go on, Ms. Kirkland."

I pushed that pesky lock of hair behind an ear and glared at Gideon, then winked with satisfaction.

"As I was saying, the office smelled what he believed in

his professional judgment to be marijuana. And upon further inspection, visual at his point, he saw two joints in between each of the fingers of the occupants of the vehicle."

"You mean to say they were just smoking them right there in the car?"

"That is correct."

"There is no proof my client was smoking his joint at the time of the arrest, Your Honor," Gideon said.

"Really, counselor?" Judge Heller responded with a raised brow.

"Yes, really. The office does not attest to witnessing my client *smoking* the joint. Only *holding* it."

The judge huffed and sat back, frowning but responding with nothing more. "Go on, Ms. Kirkland."

I cleared my throat, knowing the next part is where it got dicy. "Next, the officer instructed Pentwell and his companion to exit the vehicle, at which point he conducted a routine search of the car and discovered the large quantity of unprocessed cannabis stems inside the two shopping bags in the trunk of the car."

"Routine search my ass," Gideon complained, slapping his legal pad on the table with an amount of flair that was dramatic even for Gideon. "They were closed shut!"

"The officer had a good faith belief there was more to the story, given the two extenuating pieces of evidence."

Judge Heller furrowed his brow. "I don't know, Ms. Kirkland. Seems a bit of a stretch."

"Then what were they doing in the car with joints and the stench of marijuana pouring from the vehicle?"

Gideon scoffed. "How about going for a drive?"

I replied, "Which is still illegal in the State of Michigan, operating a vehicle and smoking a joint. Same as drinking and driving."

"She's got you there, counselor," the judge said.

"Yes, but first of all," Gideon plowed forward, "my client didn't test positive for THC because he hadn't been smoking the joint."

"Yet..." I said, rolling my eyes.

"And second," he said, glaring my way, "neither the presence of a joint nor the smell of marijuana gives the police probable cause to search the vehicle! And definitely not opening sealed bags. Neither of which violated state law. And whether there were garbage bags filled to the brim sitting in the back seat gives the police zero grounds to search the vehicle. The bags could have been filled with clothes he was going to have laundered or bring to Goodwill, even."

"But it wasn't."

"Doesn't matter," he snapped, then added: "Respectfully, Your Honor. And since the discovery leading to the charge would be considered fruit of the poisonous tree— that is, if you rule in our favor and deem the search illegal, then Mill Creek Junction has no case against my client."

Judge Heller took a breath and leaned back. "I don't know, counselor. I could go either ways on letting this go to trial."

I leaned back in my chair as well, assessing my options. It was a flip of a coin at this point. Fifty-fifty. And I would rather get a win at some level than lose to a stinkin' probable-cause ruling.

Finally, I smiled in a huff. Time to put on my big girl pants a second time, gather my dignity about me, and get out while I still could.

"Your Honor, would you mind giving me a minute with opposing counsel? Perhaps we can find a solution that would be equitable for each party, and your own time."

"Take two," said Judge Heller, then he gaveled a ten-minute recess to let him use the little boy's room.

Gideon turned toward me. "Well?"

I wanted to say, don't look so smug. But then I thought, don't poke the bear.

Instead, I said, "Two weeks of community service, no fine." It looked like he was about to object, so I added: "He was caught with almost four ounces while operating a motor vehicle, which is a clear violation of the law."

I waited for his answer. He sighed and looked off, clearly reveling in the turn of tables.

Then he nodded. "I'll take that to my client. But no record. Especially this nonsense felony intent-to-distribute charge."

I nodded back. "No record."

"Alright, then. I think we'll have a deal."

He put out his hand. I briefly eyed it, but took it.

After shaking on it, and then announcing the agreement to the judge, who gave it his blessing, I left and shuffled up to my office. Where I knew the seven-headed dragon from the Book of Revelation would not be happy.

Pushing through the wood door that was our offices, guess who was waiting?

There was this smirk that irritated the snot out of me, and he opened his arms up as if he were waiting for news of his pregnant wife's labor.

"Well?" he asked, grinning like the prick he was.

I took a breath and smiled back. "We got a deal."

His face fell, then furrowed. "Deal? What kind of deal?"

Crapola. Probably shouldn't have led with that word.

I pushed past into my office. He followed. I slung my bag on my desk and came clean, explaining what went down in court and the deal I had made with Gideon. I finished. His face darkened.

"My office," he commanded, then stormed out into the corner he'd snagged, shutting the door with restraint behind me.

"Community service?" he grumbled, moving behind his desk in some sort of macho power play.

I took a breath and raised my head. "That's right."

"Why the hell did you do that? We had the kid on intent and you know it!"

"Give me a break, Dean! You're bonkers if you think all of this was nothing more than political posturing during an election season."

"It was a matter of law, not politics, clear and simple."

"Bulldookie! It was a matter of politics, clear and simple, mister."

He folded his arms. "Then what was this deal you made about then, huh?"

I waited a beat, considering his question. Then settled on: "A matter of justice. No way we try the kid a felony for simple possession. Which is just a political hatchet job, anyway."

That seemed to give him pause. His nostrils flared like they did when he didn't get his way, and he folded his arms. A sure sign he was giving in.

Then he sat down at his desk. "Fine," he said, attending to something at his computer.

And that was that.

I left, then slunk back to my office feeling like all eyes were drilling me with suspicion and condescension and that German word that always trips me up.

Schadenfreude. That's it. That.

None of which I neither wanted nor needed. So I grabbed my purse and left for home.

The morning began with a grande extra-hot flat white with sugar-free vanilla and an extra shot. It was ending with gin and tonic.

I pulled one of my daddy's old records and put it on the turntable and struck up "In a Sentimental Mood" by John Coltrane. Seemed appropriate, given what I was feeling after that case.

Then I kicked off my pumps and slumped down hard in a hand-me-down leather chair and took a mouthful of my drink, closing my eyes and letting Coltrane's dreamy sax vibe take me away.

A matter of justice, I'd said. Most days, I believed that was the calling card of my chosen profession.

Others....Not so much.

But Coltrane might be able to change my mind.

And the gin and tonic.

"Let justice roll down like waters," the Good Book says.

Exactly.

I'll drink to that.

STORY 3

GO AND DO LIKEWISE

MAX'S PLACE was hopping like I had never seen it hopping before. Loud and lively, smelling great and feeling great.

Just what I needed...

Figured it was people finally coming out from hibernation after being cooped up from that virus nonsense earlier in the year and all the other craziness the decade's thrown Mill Creek Junction, not to mention the rest of the world. Who knew the second decade of the 21st century would be filled with pandemics and face masks, murder hornets and cicadas! And that wasn't even touching on the powder keg that was set off in cities around the country after that bastard cop suffocated George Floyd two states over. What I wouldn't give to be on that case. I'd take it pro bono, too. Would bleed Minneapolis dry after the hell they put that family through. Not like the shyster that poor family had now, bungling the thing and letting that piece of scum get off with that botched autopsy report. The two-bit lawyer who—

"Gideon, my man!" Max crowed, looking like he'd won the lottery. "Lawyer extraordinaire!"

I laughed, taking the man's open palm and following through with the embrace. "What's gotten into you? Aside from the Grey Goose, of course. You win the Mega Millions Michigan lottery, or something?"

"No, man. This!" he said, twisting up his face and pointing both thumbs his way. "I ain't had a lick of booze. Coke Zero, my man."

"Wow. Look forward to catching you once the shots start flying. What are you so amped up for then?"

"This!" he said, gesturing with wide arms and twirling. "The people, the food, the music—"

"And the bar tabs?"

He ended his twirl facing me with a wide grin. "Music to my ears."

I guess I was right about the lotto.

But he was right. Sure was nice to see Max's Place filled to the brim with familiar faces, his grill sending up seared beef and melted cheese, Burt creating some dish with saffron and mustard and salmon from the back, the jazz ensemble throwing up a modern rendition of Jimmy Smith's "The Sermon." Even my frown was being turned upside down at the lively mood.

Max slapped me on the back and guided me to the bar, where I eased into a bar chair and slumped against the polished dark wood smelling of lemon polish.

"Looks like you're back in business, buddy!" I said, slapping the guys shoulder as he moved to the back of the bar.

"More than back! My peepers can hardly believe my numbers. People sure were ready to get back to life after the corona crazy this past year."

"I guess so."

"What are you drinkin' tonight, partner?"

"Surprise me."

Max hummed with a little too much pleasure that made me think I was in for quite the treat. Or quite the ride. Either way, the drink would be more than welcomed.

I turned around toward the back where the band was striking up another tune. Sounded like the organist switched from one of Smith's earlier bluesy numbers to a later groovier one from his fusion days, the late-60s evolution in jazz when musicians combined jazz harmony and improvisation with rock and funk, with rhythm and blues. "Root Down," if he recalled. Good number, with the man on the whites-and-blacks working the ivory of the old, boxy, honey-stained contraption like it was nobody's business, the drums keeping up a nice rhythm, a youngster strumming his electric guitar, working the strings up and down with a twisted-up face that said he was feeling what the organ was putting down.

"Here you go, partner," Max said, setting down his drink with a bit of flair to the hand Gideon had come to expect.

"What's this?"

"A Man-hattin', for my man who seems to be havin' a terrible, horrible, no good, very bad day."

I chuckled, grasping the stem to the cocktail glass that seemed a bit boujee for Max's Place, which wasn't even getting at the fact Max knew how to make a Manhattan in the first place. Much more a pint and bottle sort of place and sort of guy, but whatever.

The bourbon and sweet vermouth would do me a world of good.

I eyed it before its maiden voyage. "Did you manage a dash of Angostura and orange bitters and all?"

"Even garnished it with a brandied cherry," Max said with a grin, bobbing back and forth on the balls of his heels with pride.

I tipped my non-existent hat to the man then took a sip.

Closing my eyes and sighing with pleasure, mellow with the slightest hint of that brandied cherry, the bitters bringing the bourbon and vermouth together in a perfect tango, slightly bitter and herbal with an underlying sweetness and headiness that was already working its magic.

Heaven.

"Look what the cat dragged in," a voice called from behind.

I sucked in a breath at its familiarity, praying it wasn't so.

I spun toward my left, not seeing anyone. Then I got a tap on my right shoulder. So I spun back to confirm my dreadful suspicions.

Annabelle Kirkland. Assistant Prosecuting Attorney for Mill Creek Junction. My chief rival.

Heaven to hot Hades in a flash.

She sidled up to my right, pulling out a chair.

"Annabelle," I said. "Fancy seeing you here. Thought you'd be burning the midnight oil putting the finishing touches on your closing arguments for some trial."

"I finished those hours ago. Hence Max's Place."

"Hey there, sweetheart," Max interrupted, grinning like a boy neck deep in puberty. "You joining the cowboy here?"

She glanced my way, giving me eyes full of question marks. I shrugged and gestured with my head toward the open seat.

She smiled and took it. "I guess so."

He slapped one of his coasters down in front, a surprising thing I hadn't noticed before.

I picked it up and squinted in the dim bar light, the bar colophon with some sort of slogan.

"Serving bull since 1918?" I said, twisting up my face toward Max, who was pulling a draft for Annabelle.

"Ahh, yes. The new additions to the joint," he said, finishing and snatching it back from my fingers before slapping it back down in front of Annabelle and setting her drink down with an even more dramatic flourish than mine.

"What was wrong with the old ones?"

"What, those bland, run-of-the-mill thingies with the Miller or Bud logos that every other greasy spoon has?"

I shrugged. Man had a point. "But, serving bull?"

He grinned and leaned forward. "That was my little turn of phrase. Like it?"

Annabelle snorted a laugh. "I think it's super, Max. The whole double entendre thing you got going on there with it."

His grin widened, his eyes brightening and face reddening slightly at the attention. "I thought it was pretty clever myself."

"But you don't serve bull, do you? Your burgers are just cow beef, aren't they?"

Max's face fell, and he huffed a frustrated breath. "The double entendre don't work if you say 'Serving beef patties since 1918,' genius!"

I threw back a swig and shook my head. "Has a nice ring to it though."

He scoffed and threw a rag at me, which I caught with one hand.

"Pay him no mind, Max," Annabelle said. "Real original, it is."

"It is pretty good," I finally agreed. "And I'll witness to

regular amounts of bull being served from behind that bar top, that's for sure!"

The same rag was thrown, and I dodged it just in time, the thing sailing past and hitting someone else in the back of the head.

Max grimaced and went to duck before he was caught by whoever it was he had hit. He left us in peace to make up for his goof.

"Ah, Max. God love him." I took another swig of the Manhattan, the glass nearly empty now, hoping the man would be back soon to refill.

"You do have to admit, it was pretty clever," Annabelle said.

That it was. And that was Max. Sometimes a little too clever for his own good.

"So what brings you here tonight?" she asked, crushing a peanut from a red basket Max kept up at the bar, popping it in her mouth.

I drained my Manhattan and pushed the glass forward, just as Max returned. I asked for whatever he pulled for Annabelle.

I leaned back and sighed, a headache beginning to needle the middle part of my head. "Not to be rude or anything, but I'm not really in the mood, Annabelle."

She took a swig of her beer, but continued: "Heard about the Lopez case. Sorry about that."

My stomach sank at the reminder, how I had inadvertently gotten the migrant and his family yanked by ICE after taking his case to recoup back pay and lost wages from one of the local celery farms. How was I to know the guy wasn't here illegally—or rather, undocumented?

"Can I ask you something?" Annabelle asked, leaning closer, her movement whipping up the scent of lavender.

Had never noticed her scent in that way before. Never much thought about it, either.

But I liked it...

Max set down one of his coasters in front of me this time before setting down the beer. I nodded and threw back a swig.

"Shoot," I said.

"Why did you get into this?"

I looked around the room dumbly, as if not understanding. "Max's Place?"

She frowned and hit my arm. "No, silly. The law! Your own personal practice."

"Ahh, that." I shrugged. "Same as anyone else. The money."

She laughed. "On the cases you try? Immigration violators, bail jumpers—shoot that pothead son of that Junction councilwoman?"

I took another swig, running through my answer.

Which I had. Always had, but had never really voiced to anyone.

Until now. Maybe.

I swallowed again and turned toward her, eying her with skepticism. After all, she was the Mill Creek Junction APA.

Ahh, what the hell. Why not. Maybe it would build a bridge I could use down the road. Whether in a case she was trying or something deeper...

I turned toward her, my movement throwing up another whiff of that lavender, the light catching her strawberry hair and hazel eyes and button nose and red lips in a way I hadn't noticed before. I mean, yeah, I noticed. But not like that. Maybe it was something about the way she was asking about my interest in the law, about why I did what I did.

The way she was asking about me. Seeing me, even.

My mouth was suddenly running dry, so I asked Max for a glass of water. I took a swig of my beer, then another. Then dove in with both feet, my palms sweating but not caring a lick.

Here we go...

"So get this. One day, my pops and I are driving into town. Just got off I-96 and made the turn onto Main Street when the reds and blues start flashing."

She giggled. "Yeah, my daddy got pulled over a time or two down in Memphis. I think I was nine the first time it happened. He told me to shut up and let him do all the talking. I was scared out of my wits! How old were you?"

"About the same age. Maybe less. So Pops pulls over. The cop gets out and starts crunching across the gravel. This was before Main Street saw pavement. And it was one of those West Michigan scorchers. Sun high and sky cloudless. Lake Michigan receding after a dry spell that spelled doom for the celery and onions wilting at the edge of town."

I took another large mouthful of beer, draining it and nodding to Max for another as he set down my water. But something stronger this time. Top shelf.

Because I was gonna need it for what came next.

"So what happened?" she asked, leaning in with one end of her mouth curled upward.

Oh, sister. If you only knew what was coming.

Max fished out a bottle of Maker's Mark and poured two finger's worth, then another when I motioned for him to keep at it.

Throwing back a swig, I answered, "What happened was, Pops kept his hands on the steering wheel and told me not to say a word. Not to move. I can still hear the crunch of those boots on that gravel. Dry as a dog in heat."

"OK...then what?" she asked.

"Then the cop reaches my dad's door. He'd already had the window rolled down, since it was one of those summer afternoons. And when he reached it, he startled."

"Startled?"

"Yeah. Startled. There was this double skip of the cop's boots on the bone-dry gravel that gave it away. A skip and a hop. Skip, hop."

I threw back another swig and swallowed hard, the smokey amber liquid sliding down with a pleasurable burn that made telling the tale all the easier.

"And after that, his hand went to his sidearm."

"His sidearm?" Annabelle exclaimed, reaching for her own drink and tossing some back in the chute. "What for? It was a simple traffic stop, for crying out loud."

I grinned, then shook my head. Simple traffic stop.

"That's right. The guy put his hand on the holster of his sidearm, then unclipped the flap holding it in place. I can still remember that slight unsnapping. Sounded like the brass button on my jeans when I went to take them off."

Another swig. More fuel to get me through.

"Anyway, so yeah, he's getting ready—"

"For what? It was a cotton pickin' traffic stop!"

You're telling me, sister.

"For what came next," I said.

Then I took a breath. And another swig, draining the scotch and nodding to Max for more.

He raised a brow, as if confirming.

I nodded, giving confirmation.

He shrugged and twisted off the red-wax cap and poured a generous amount.

Which was both nice and needed.

"For what came next..." Annabelle said, voice betraying impatience. "Which was?"

I took a breath, then dove in: "He took a step back, that bone-dry gravel throwing up a wicked crunch again, before raising his weapon and pointing it at Dad. Then he ordered him out."

Annabelle sucked in a startled breath, almost like a balloon wheezing unexpectedly, but in the opposite direction.

I glanced at her, taking another swig of scotch and really feeling it now. She had a small hand raised to her mouth. Which she let fall with conscious realization when she saw me glance up.

"So Pops whispered a few words to me," I went on, "then popped the lock to his door, eased it open on creaking hinges, and stepped out onto that bone-dry shoulder, his polished black leather shoes clacking against the road."

All of it was coming at me in technicolor, high-definition precision. The sights and sounds and details still crisply sitting in the synapses of my brain and dredged to the surface by my trusty hippocampus.

"What did you do?" she whispered. "What were you...feeling?"

What was I feeling? A question I'd never really contemplated before.

But then my hippocampus threw up one more detail. Well, two, which were tied together.

"I wet myself, if that tells you anything." I left it there and threw back another swig of Maker's Mark, that wet sensation and salty stench as real as the day it all went down.

Another wheezing squeak from Annabelle before the

band drowned out any more with another Jimmy Smith number. Something from "Back at the Chicken Shack."

I smiled at the organ striking a jiving boogie before a snare started up and tenor saxophone took over. One of Dad's favorite albums. Seemed a bit ironic. A bit providential, even. As if the universe was sending up a sign or something.

I took a breath and continued: "Anyway, so Dad stepped out, and before he knew it, he was on the ground, his forehead smacking into the gravel road."

I hit the bar top with a *smack!* Then again: SMACK!

I could tell Annabelle jumped, but didn't apologize. The copper certainly hadn't.

"And then the cop said—"

My tongue stumbled over itself, choking on the words and the memory, righteous indignation welling from my belly. Whether from the memory itself or its retelling or goaded by Maker's Mark, I wasn't sure. Either way, what came next wasn't pretty.

And it was godawful hard...

"Don't even think about moving, the cop said," I went on, "Because no way no Junction judge will give two snots if a nappy coon takes one to the back of the head."

A gasp escaped her a beat later, popping through a final handoff between Jimmy Smith and Stanley Turrentine on the tenor sax again, as if she understood the full measure of it all.

As if she understood me, understood my *story* in all of its fullness—a detail not everyone got.

We sat that way for a while, in silence and stillness. In recognition.

I took in a measured breath, the words of that white cop slung at my adoptive father continuing to marinate between us as another jazz number was struck up. That newfangled Kamasi Washington that was all the rage. Liked the guy, but his notes hit flat, mixed with my sour memory.

"Wait..." Annabelle finally said. "Your parents are—"

"Black. African American, as the kids say nowadays." I drained my glass and swallowed, setting it down with a thud.

She gawped for words. Which was all at once cute and annoying. As if white people were the only ones who could adopt outside their race, and not the other way around.

"I'm adopted, in case you couldn't tell." I offered a weak smile that probably came across as cocky and condescending.

But then a hand came to my leg. "I had no idea."

"About what? My family's racial incident or my family's racial makeup?"

Again, way more cocky and condescending than I intended, and that was necessary. I blamed the Maker's Mark.

And the memory.

She withdrew her hand. I felt horrible.

So I said, "Sorry. You didn't need your head bitten off like that."

She offered a smile. "Then can I have it back, please?"

I chuckled, making a motion toward her as if I were handing it back.

She put it on like a hat. We shared another laugh.

"Seriously, though, I didn't know your parents were African American. Certainly didn't know about that racial incident with the cops. And I'm sorry that's part of your story—part of your *dad's* story."

"That ain't the only one, sweetheart..." I mumbled, draining my scotch and then taking in some water. "And that's why I'm in this. To defend people like my dad from people like that cop."

"That makes sense..." she said, finishing her own drink.

"So what about you?" I said, throwing on a smile and turning in my chair.

"What about me what?"

"Why'd you get into the law?"

She glanced at her watch, then twisted up her face into a smirk and flagged down Max. "Now *that* is another story for another time. Max," she called out toward the man a few tables over. He came over and she asked for her tab.

"Wait a minute," I said, looking at Max head for the register before returning to Annabelle. "I just told you my life story and you're bailing on me?"

She started gathering her things. "Sorry. I really am. Leaving you high and dry after you basically poured your heart out. But I've got a big case tomorrow that I need to prep for."

"Not me I hope."

"No, not you."

Max brought Annabelle her tab, and she handed over her credit card, shrugging at me as he cashed her out.

"But hey, let me tell you something my granddad told me growing up. Something from the Bible, actually."

"Are you seriously going to quote Scripture to me right now? Here of all places?"

She shrugged. "It's a Southern thing."

I scoffed. "And a West Michigan thing. But alright. Go on."

She slung her purse at her lap and said, "So Jesus tells this story, a parable, about three men who passed by a hurting man on the side of the road who had been robbed."

I smiled and nodded. "Oh, yeah. The Parable of the

Good Samaritan. I remember hearing about that as a kid growing up at Mill Creek Junction Baptist. About the priest, the Levite, and the Samaritan, isn't that right?"

"Look at you! All Johnny-on-the-spot with Bible trivia."

"I'm not as much of a heathen as you might think I am."

"Anyway, as you know, the priest and Levite passed by the poor soul, but the Samaritan didn't. He stopped and helped him out. Patched him up and paid for his medical care. And Jesus asked the expert in the law who had been pestering him which of the three was a neighbor to the poor soul stranded on the side of the road."

"Right, the Samaritan, the guy answered."

"Well, technically, he said the one who had mercy on the man, but that's not the point."

I raised a brow. "Then what is?"

Max handed back her card, along with her receipt and a pen. She offered her John Hancock, then pointed at my chest and said, "You're that guy."

"What guy?"

"The Good Samaritan. Jesus said, *'Go and do likewise.'* In other words, engage in neighbor-love, wherever you find it. And it sounds like you took his teachings to heart."

I furrowed up my brow with confusion, then let it fall, accepting her words with a small measure of pride. Not sure I agreed with her, that I'd taken Jesus' teachings to heart and all. In fact, I know I'd forsaken most of them, a small measure of guilt rising within. But her kind words somehow gave me comfort after a day I felt like a complete failure.

Go and do likewise. Pretty wise advice. Something I'd take with me. And from my chief rival, no less.

"Anyway," she said. "I should be going."

She stood, as did I. Didn't know why. Sorta just happened. And then I blurted: "Hey, if you're gonna stand me up like this, not telling me how you got into the law and all, then you owe me a second round."

"A second round?"

"A date," I said, my head not keeping up with my tongue. Or maybe it was my heart. Either way, I was as surprised as the look on her face.

"Not that this was a date or anything," I quickly said, trying to recover. "All I mean to say is that you owe me your story. Especially after spilling my guts just now."

She seemed to catch her breath. But then she smiled, pushing a lock of stray strawberry blond hair behind those small ears of hers, those white chiclet teeth at the front that always seemed to short circuit my brain in court popping through.

"Alright, Gideon O'Donnell, it's a deal." She hoisted up her massive purse and stuck out her hand.

I eyed it, disappointed she wasn't in the mood to embrace. But it was about all I was going to get. After all, we were still chief rivals.

One end of my mouth curled upward, and I took it. "Deal."

"Goodnight," she said as she turned to leave.

But then she stopped, turning back and adjusting that massive purse on those slight shoulders of hers. She said, "Thanks for sharing, Gideon. Yourself. I mean, some of your story," she quickly said, as if recovering. "It was nice."

I nodded. "And thanks for listening. It was nice."

"Let's do it again sometime."

"And soon," I said, rushing a bit too quickly, but my tongue was well beyond controlling at that point. "I mean, we did shake on it and all."

She smiled and said, "Deal," before leaving and walking out into the night.

I watched the door thud shut, and continued watching her walk past the big picture window anchoring the front, grateful to have shared part of my story.

With her.

Go and do likewise. Engage in neighbor-love.

I liked the sound of that.

STORY 4

WHERE'S THE JUSTICE?

"MADAM FOREPERSON," Judge Joey Heller said, "have you reached a verdict?"

There was a scuffing of chairs against the wood floor to my left and a shuffling of feet. The defendant stood, along with his pair of attorneys.

I scooted to the edge of my seat. Couldn't help it. Acted out of habit. A ritual I had performed since joining the Prosecuting Attorney's office a few years ago after moving to Mill Creek Junction from Knoxville, Tennessee. No one knew why in my right mind I'd do such a thing.

But I had my reasons.

One of them was prosecuting murderers who killed their adulterous spouses.

And now I was waiting for the verdict to a homicide case that should have been an easy guilty verdict, without question if the sun didn't shine and the creek didn't rise, as my meemaw always said.

Yet there had been issues. Things I hadn't anticipated. Things Annabelle Kirkland wasn't in the habit of transgressing under normal circumstances.

For one, that devilish defense attorney, Gideon O'Donnell, snatching up the case. Although, looking back, it made sense and should I have definitely anticipated that one, given his penchant for defending Junction lowlifes.

But he had been the least of my worries. And the least of my problems.

"What do you think, Kirkland?" Dean Lawlor asked in a rushed whisper, leaning forward against the wooden rail at my back.

Speaking of said problems.

My boss's mitts had been all over the case from the start. For good reason, I suppose. Where one of the Junction's councilmen is found passed out like a drunk skunk on Main Street by one of Mill Creek's finest, brows are liable to be raised.

Especially when they're part of Mayor Goodall's political party.

Damn small-town politics.

Doubly so when the officer brought the drunkard home only to find his front door flapping in the wind. And the body of his wife from inspecting the premises after the alarming front door. A true Shakespearian tragedy is what he found inside. Then when Councilman Peterson's story didn't add up, things took a decidedly Shakespearian turn that landed me riding shotgun with various law enforcement muckety-mucks after I'd been picked from the pool of other APA grunts when my number had been drawn from a fish bowl.

And on a case a pinch beyond my means. Of course, I never expressed such sentiments to Dean. Would have been career suicide. Especially once the press piled onboard the crazy train, attracting the attention of major media outlets from Sea to Shining Sea, there was no way I could say no.

So I strapped my big girl boots on, saddled up, and dug my spurs into the horsey, taking off down Main Street and straight into hell.

That was a month ago. And now I was sitting at the edge of my seat, shaking a pinch in my proverbial cowgirl boots, and waiting for that darned Jury Foreperson to get to it already while Dean was breathing at the back of my neck. Literally, the smell of that kielbasa with extra onions still clinging to his hot breath.

I shifted, nearly sliding off my chair but catching myself with the heel of my lucky red pumps glossed red like the lipstick of a fine southern belle. Which fit the bill to a T, in my humble opinion.

Had a good feeling about this one. No way a jury would move for a dismissal after the evidence we presented.

Well, not so much the evidence as the nature of the crime itself, for there had been a pinch of trouble on that front.

Like I said: a true Shakespearean tragedy.

The first sign of trouble was the door itself. Unlocked. No sign of forced entry, no splintered jamb or broken glass, as if the occupant of the house knew the perp standing at the front door. Or the perp came from inside the house itself, only to later flee and binge-drink his life away down Main Street. Which is pretty much what I argued.

The second sign of trouble was the bloody handprint. Or rather, prints. And streaks. Up and down the walls in curving arcs leading up a staircase to the second floor. It was as if a toddler had popped the top to a can of Sherwin-Williams and gooped the crimson stuff all over the wall, it was so bad!

Legitimately alarmed at this point, the officer instructed

the councilman to remain in the car for his own safety before heading up for a look-see.

Someone cleared their throat before sighing from want of an answer, sending up another whiff of kielbasa-covered onion breath. "Well?"

The stench combined with my tightening gut almost made me lose my lunch then and there.

I went to answer when the clompy shoes of an old woman thudded against the scuffed courthouse wood floor.

A pinched face woman, her silver hair spun up into a wicked bun rose to unstable feet, a dress looking more like a picnic table cloth falling to her shins.

Madam Foreperson.

Reminded me of my meemaw from the Deep South. As in Georgia Deep.

"We have, your honor," Madam Foreperson announced in a shrill tone that set my teeth on edge.

"Well?" Dean asked again in the same whispered rush. "Should we make the deal?"

"No!" I said with more conviction than I had, matching his same whispered rush, but adding a pinched brow and a raised corner to my upper lip that told him to back off.

He did, slinking back into the walnut wood bench that had been his perch for the last few weeks of trial.

Surprising, really, when I think about it. That the man hadn't taken first chair, or even second chair, given the highly publicized—not to mention the highly *politicized*—nature of the whole bloomin' thing. But the jury consultants said it would play better if a woman ran the show, given the grizzly nature of what the councilman had been accused of. And Dean in the second chair would only muddy the waters of waters that had been soaked in blood—literally, in the case of the victim, Penelope Peterson.

After clearing the main floor of any threat, and finding no victim, the attending officer proceeded up the stairs to the second floor, following the crimson-streaked wall toward destiny. Clearing all other rooms, he opened the door to the master bedroom.

And found nothing.

Not a drop of blood on the carpet. Not a misplaced pillow or rumpled sheet on the bed, which was still made. No broken glass or torn curtains or toppled nightstand.

Nothing.

Except for a ribbon of light cutting through the cracked bathroom door.

Which he proceeded toward. Then opened.

Finding a white-marbled toilet room covered in blood. Painted. Like the kiddo who'd cracked the can of Sherwin-Williams crimson.

And then the body.

Floating in water-color red, the kind of water leftover from the same kiddo who had spent a morning painting with Crayola paints. Penelope's throat was slashed open. Not once, not twice. But three times.

Hence all the Sherwin-Williams covering the bathroom, and then streaking down the stairwell wall to the main floor.

But oddly, not visible on the councilman.

Which made sense, to some degree, since the man was found hammered on a Main Street curb.

But those two competing details had bothered me from the start.

Lots of blood; no blood.

Wife slaughtered like one of Grandpappy's pigs; husband passed out on Main Street. The guy hadn't even been to Max's Place. I'd checked, three times; we all had. So why had he been three sheets to the wind?

I showed up fifteen minutes after I got the call, and with the councilman still in the back of the officer's car. Passed out. Dean was out of town across state at some muckety-muck meeting of state prosecuting attorneys, so I was on call.

At first, we treated him as a grieving, newly widowed man. Or rather *later*, once he came to, given the state of the man's intoxication.

But then we wondered. Especially since Chief Roller, who had been managing the crime scene, had heard it through the grapevine that Penelope had been less than faithful with some auto parts store owner across town. Apparently, she was trading up the vocational food chain. And might have paid the price.

Which gave us motive. And opportunity, given the pair were husband and wife, so he certainly had access to the victim. And the fact the man had been drunk off his ass, an obvious sign of acute emotional trauma from an act few of us would be able to handle—and, well, $1 + 1 + 1$ equalled a definite suspect.

So, with the man passed out in the back seat, I instructed the chief to take him back to the Junction police department for questioning. And we did.

Which I would later realize was a mistake. And Dean wouldn't let me forget once he got his mitts on the case.

Sitting him in an interrogation room of sanitized-white light and tiles, steel table and chair bolted to the floor, we got to work. We hadn't handcuffed him, since we didn't view him as a risk, and neither did we Mirandize him, since he wasn't technically a suspect. It was a friendly chat with the drunk husband of a dead wife trying to get some clarifying answers.

Still nearly groggy from the alcohol and weeping from

having been told his wife had been murdered, we got him a large cup of coffee to preference—two creams, two sugars. The crime scene detective, Jamie Roscoe, handed the man his coffee and got to work. I watched from my typical perch, behind mirrored plexiglass as the woman stepped up to the plate and began to slowly edge the man toward a confession.

The woman was a top-notch investigator as far as I was concerned from previous experience. Seemed a bit over-eager around a crime scene though, a thick stomach and even thicker skin who gave herself with abandon to her work. Not that I thought she had some weirdy-woo fascination with dead things or gore. More like I admired her for the way she could handle herself around such hopelessness, around the end result of Mama Eve and Papa Adam's transgressions against the Almighty back in the Garden: the full-on depravity of the human heart displayed through severed heads and broken limbs, violent sexual assault, and bathtubs full of diluted blood spewing from necks slashed thrice over.

There was a part of me that thought we should Mirandize the man, wondering if he would give us anything that might work and worried that if he did we'd be in hot doo-doo legally. But I let it pass, fearing the man would lawyer up as he sobered up and realized we were homing in on him as suspect numero uno.

Roscoe began leaning into his reason for drinking, reason for hanging around Main Street. Peterson said he had had a bad day and needed to blow off steam.

I bet.

She pressed him, asking him about leaving the house—when and why he left the door open. He didn't know when, thought he'd shut the door on his way out.

Then she moved to questions about his wife: What was

she doing when he left; he didn't know. Was she upstairs in the bathtub; he didn't know. What was her demeanor like before he left; seemed fine, but they didn't speak much. Any known associates who might want to harm her, or unknown ones who would want to harm her, enemies and such; he didn't know. Was she alive when he left for his jaunt down Main Street drunk off his ass, or was she conscious when he slashed her throat three times?

Actually, that's what I wanted to ask, but never got a chance to.

It wasn't until the door to the observation deck thudded open halfway through the interview that things took a turn. The arresting officer handed me a printout he had just gotten from a lab technician on site. Apparently, while Peterson was passed out in the back of the officer's patrol car, the man took it upon himself to swab the underside of his fingernails for DNA when he took Peterson's blood alcohol level reading.

That was definitely bordering on Fourth Amendment violations, given he hadn't voluntarily offered the evidence and there hadn't been a warrant for said evidence. Judges tend to be sticklers about American citizens having the right to secure their person, even the underside of their fingernails.

However—and this is where my Southern-breed ethics and religious upbringing began creeping up my spine—the test came back a match for Ms. Peterson.

And sodium hypochlorite.

Also known as bleach.

I was not happy to have this evidence without the proper procedures, but I put my big girl boots back on and marched into the interview room with the officer. It was enough to press forward with an arrest, and we did, and I'd deal with the fallout in the courtroom.

Annabelle Kirkland style.

The man's sobbing returned right before he flashed a rageful yawp that nearly took my head off, literally. The officer had to restrain the man as he came at me with a red face and raised fist.

Had a flashback from back in Knoxville that nearly sent me scurrying out of the room. After all, it was the reason I moved up to this godforsaken land in the first place.

Then he did something unexpected: he confessed.

Raging: "That no good, cheating wife had it coming with what she'd done to me. Embarrassing me like that, making me the talk of town. And with an auto parts store owner!"

His face was nearly purple with rage, he was so mad— his arms rippling under the strength of the officer's restraint, his silvering hair standing on edge and a corkscrew vein popping at his temple from his display of vengeance.

Wasn't quite a confession, but his admission could be played many ways.

One of which was probable cause.

I held it together, stepping back toward the man and withholding a gleeful grin after what I'd just been handed. Never bite the hand that feeds you, Mama always said. Or gloat when a psychopathic, murdering husband basically confesses to his crime. I read him his rights as he was cuffed, and that was that. He went limp, probably from resigned understanding, and was hauled out to spend the night in lock up.

Then the real work began.

The work of proving what we thought to be true.

That the man murdered his wife in a rageful fit after discovering she had cheated on him—and with an auto parts store owner, no less; the rageful fit displayed in the interview room certainly fit the bill—then drank himself into a remorseful stupor before stumbling down Main Street and passing out.

Between the DNA and the circumstantial evidence, compounded by the near-confession admission, it was definitely enough to work with.

The next day after Peterson was booked, he was brought before a different judge than Heller for arraignment—with Gideon and his sidekick Reggi Wilson in tow.

I charged the councilman with first degree murder, then attached second degree as a lesser included offense, given the nature of the crime. Although premeditation was a dicey proposition to prove, we thought there was solid enough evidence to get him on it. I also pushed for no bail, given the nature of the crime.

To which Gideon loudly and dramatically objected.

"Your Honor," he said, "My client is an upstanding member of the community, a councilman for god's sake, who poses little risk to the Junction and carries little flight risk."

"I'm sorry," I retorted, "but since when does nearly decapitating one's wife and letting her blood in a bathtub of hot water not pose a danger to the community?"

"Objection, Your Honor!" Gideon said.

"And since when do we allow murderers of any sort to roam freely up and down Main Street, even and especially politically well-connected ones?"

"Oh, come on! Should we just convict the man now without even a jury—"

"Alright, alright, you two," the judge interrupted with a

staying hand to us both. "Two counts of murder are rendered, bail set at one million dollars."

He dropped his gavel before T could interject, and Peterson was hauled away. But not before his lawyer stepped back up to the plate.

"Your honor, at this time we move for a suppression hearing to suppress as evidence any confession or admission given by the defendant while in custody."

"On what ground?" I asked.

"On the ground that it was involuntary."

"Are you high—"

"Alright, alright, you two," the judge interjected again. "The judge assigned to the case is Heller, so you may submit your motion with him."

Then he gaveled us again, and we were dismissed.

Not good...

Round one went to Gideon, which wasn't the biggest thing to lose. But there is a momentum element to trials. And you want the Big Mo on your side from the start. So losing bail was not a good way to start. Then to know a suppression motion was coming was really not good—considering how shady it all went down.

But I figured we would see. And the next morning we did.

"All rise," the court officer intoned. "This court is now in session by the honorable Judge Joseph Z. Heller."

"Yes, yes, yes," the man said before settling his thin frame into his overly large black leather chair, "be seated, and what not."

The man sure had a curious way about him.

"What business is being brought before me this morning?"

Gideon stood and announced, "Gideon O'Donnell,

representing Councilman Gerald Peterson. And we come bearing a motion to suppress."

I flashed him a wry grin from across the aisle. Come bearing?

"And what motion is it you, well, come bearing?"

"His confession. At trial it is wholly unreliable and coerced, given it was made by the defendant while so intoxicated by alcohol that he lacked the mental capacity to make it voluntarily."

I folded my arms and shook my head, muttering: "This is real rich, even for you Gideon."

Heller *ahh-hemmed* and glared at me before motioning for Gideon to continue.

"I call the court's attention to the fact that the evidence indicates the defendant was obviously intoxicated during the time the arrest took place and throughout the interview and interrogation. Consequently, the court should find the defendant was not mentally competent to waive his constitutional rights at any point. On top of that, we move to suppress the DNA evidence gathered while my defendant was passed out."

Now I stood. "This is a waste of the court's time, Your Honor! Routine DNA swabs are common police procedure and the fact the man was three sheets to the wind isn't a matter of law. The councilman was fully cognizant and aware of his surroundings during the duration of his interrogation and was well aware of what was happening at the time he all but admitted to butchering his wife!"

"Oh, come on! He admitted nothing. And besides, it was basically coerced, given his drunken state. And in no way, shape, or form did my client give consent to have his person searched and his DNA seized, much less have the option to assert his 5th Amendment right against self-incrimination!"

Heller made a sound behind pursed lips and waved a hand. Then he leaned back and stroked his scrawny bare chin before saying: "I must say, Mr. O'Donnell, I must agree somewhat with the prosecutor, here. What precedent do you have for such a maneuver?"

"People v. Knedler, Colorado 2014, found that a defendant's level of intoxication at the time of the Miranda advisement is relevant to a waiver's validity, and that he may be so intoxicated that he could not have made a knowing and intelligent waiver—"

"But it ultimately concluded," I interjected, "that the totality of the circumstances adequately established that Knedler's decision to waive his rights was informed and deliberate."

Gideon gave me a sideways glance, to which I smirked and held my head high. Yes, I did know Knedler, so take that Gideon!

"Yes, Ms. Kirkland, that is true," Judge Heller said, tapping his nose while looking down through those tiny spectacles clinging to the end of it in that way I had always found annoying. "But I don't find the totality of the circumstances adequately establishes Peterson's decision to waive his rights through his self-confession was informed and deliberate."

I sucked in an audible breath. "Excuse me?"

"That's right. I'm granting the defendant's motion to suppress."

I heard that cotton pickin' defense attorney offer a smirk of success of his own next to me as I was still processing the knuckle-headed ruling.

"In that case, Your Honor," Gideon said, "I move for an immediate dismissal, given the fruit of the poisonous tree doctrine would surely be at play here."

"Is not!" I objected, stomping a foot to put an exclamation point on my exclamation. "We have crime scene evidence and eyewitness testimony that will place the defendant at the victim's residence."

"You mean his own house?" Gideon said.

"We also found secondary trace elements of the victim's DNA on the defendant—"

"Trace elements—they were married for god's sake! Of course you'd find—"

"Can I finish?"

"No!"

"Yes, yes, yes," Judge Heller interjected. "You both have mounted a vigorous rebuttal, but I've heard enough. The motion to dismiss is denied. I find enough cause to proceed. Trial starts in a week."

Before that weasely little defense attorney could throw his perfectly coiffed hair back into the ring, we were both gaveled out.

Then the race was on to find the crime scene evidence and eyewitness testimony I needed to put that SOB in jail for life.

And I did. Footprints left behind from the councilman in the bathroom put him at the scene. At least his shoe size and shoe print. Miraculously, the traces of blood under his fingernails, as well as the trace chemical compound of bleach, got admitted by the skin of my teeth. The Supreme Court had ruled such routine non-invasive swabbing didn't violate the 4th amendment, though I wasn't so sure. What was that Lord Tennyson quote? Ours not to reason why, ours but to do and die.

Or, in my case, plow forward with my case in the hopes of nailing a conviction.

And plow forward I did, presenting all our evidence before the jury. Presenting the eyewitness testimony I promised of a neighbor hearing raised voices, then a long string of silence, hours in fact before the councilman came stumbling out of his house drunk off his ass, leaving the door wide open. Testimony of the affair, roping the John in on the action and putting him up on the stand for all to see and hear, combined with the testimony of the arresting officer who had heard the man moaning and groaning something fierce in the back seat of his patrol car, as well as an inter-esting set of seven words that was admitted, yet amounted to a confession on top of the one that had been suppressed.

'I can't believe my baby is gone.'

Boy, oh, boy, did I replay and replay and replay those seven words till they set the jury's teeth on edge!

'I can't believe my baby is gone.'

And that's how I ended. With that testimony of the officer who found the councilman nearly passed out on Main Street and blubbering those words, that was as near a confession we could get admitted.

But...

And there was a big but there...because reasonable doubt still held.

Gideon was good. Had to give credit where credit was due. He had poked holes in the DNA evidence, posed hypotheticals with the medical examiner, raised all sorts of possibilities with the eyewitness who had heard it all from their perch on Cherry Street and the arresting officer that the man could have been mourning the loss of his marriage after drinking half a bottle of Courvoisier cognac after she confessed her undying love for the auto parts manager from across town. He was so good even I thought I could be the killer!

"Very well," Judge Heller said. "What say you?"

I was shaken from replaying the whole sordid tale from the past few weeks, scooting to the edge of my seat again, that glossy red heel beginning to bob up and down with anticipation.

Time seemed to stop. Which I used to my advantage to scan the other eleven plucked from Mill Creek Junction's finest pool of people less savvy enough to get out of jury duty.

"No," I said with a whisper back. "I think we've got this one."

"In the matter of the People versus Gerald Peterson—"

"Are you sure?" he whispered again.

Not really. But if the jury didn't convict, then humanity was done for.

"—in the matter of murder in the first degree, we, the jury, find the defendant—"

Moment of truth.

"Not guilty."

All the air sucked out of the room with a gasp. Even Judge Heller looked surprised. Then there were those who were whimpering with revulsion at the injustice, Junction friends and their two grown college-age children.

I just sat, unmoving with statue-still shock, feeling like I had metastasized into the scuffed wooden chair polished with a palmful of lemon wax.

I felt a hand rest gently on my shoulder and a presence bend toward my ear.

But I didn't move. Didn't respond. I was still too stunned to offer anything.

"You win some, you lose some, Annabelle."

I startled from the familiar voice, heat beginning to rise up the back of my neck from that cotton pickin' defense attorney thinking he could jaw it up with me after that tragic miscarriage of justice.

In fact, I jolted so much from the sudden realization Gideon O'Donnell was sticking his win in my face that I stood and spun toward him, the chair flying out from underneath me and thudding against the back railing with an echo that caused even Gideon to startle backward.

I wanted to slap that smirk of that pretty little face of his.

But I didn't.

I held steady, held my hand.

Until I didn't.

I picked up the only thing I could lay my hands on.

A glass of water.

Until it wasn't in my hands any longer.

The water, not the glass.

Before I knew it, the man's face was wet, and the front of that nice navy pin-stripe suit coat of his was soaked as well.

The room gasped, then a few chuckles were heard.

And then I felt another arm gently tugging me toward a retreating position.

"Come on, Kirkland," Dean said. "Not worth it."

I took a breath and spun in the aisle toward the exit, making no contact with the man, who I was embarrassed to admit got my goat, as he brushed away the water from his suit. Saying nothing, I strode across the scuffed wood floor and out the back exit. I went to make a mad dash up the marble stairs to my office floor when Dean grabbed my arm again and led me toward the courthouse exit.

"I think a drink is in order after that one."

I went to object but had to agree. So we left out the back and made the trek to Max's Place a few blocks over. Thankfully, the place was empty. We took a pair of seats at the empty bar and ordered two scotches, neat.

Sheila placed our drinks in front of us, and we each took a swig in silence. I took another straight away, then held back, staring at the clean glasses arrayed across from us on dark wood shelves from a century ago.

"Where's the justice..." I finally mumbled, throwing back the rest of my scotch and tapping my glass for a second round.

"What was that?" Dean asked, taking another swig himself.

"I said where's the justice?"

He scoffed. "Beats the hell out of me." He drained the rest of his own scotch and asked Sheila for more of the same.

I turned to him. "You know, a line from Scripture comes to mind."

Dean put up a staying hand. "Whoa, whoa, whoa. Not sure about quoting the Bible mid-afternoon after the first round of scotch. Wait for round two."

I couldn't help but giggle. As Sheila set his drink down, I said: "Now may I quote you some Bible?"

He nodded. "Bottom's up..."

We each threw back a swig. Then I said, "'*Hate evil and love good,*' Amos chapter 5 says, '*and maintain justice in the courts—*'"

"'*Perhaps the Lord God Almighty will be with you...*'"

My mouth dropped. "I declare, Dean Lawlor. Didn't take you for the Scripture-quoting type."

"Hey, I'm not all heathen!" He took a sip and continued, "And Lord help us here in the Junction, given what just went down in that courthouse. Because he ain't with us after that!"

I smirked and took a small sip myself, then said quietly: "Agree."

Now Dean turned to me. "Listen, Annabelle, you win some, you lose some."

I scoffed and threw back another swig. "That's what Gideon mouthed off to me, right before I doused him."

He laughed. "That was pretty good of you."

"And satisfying," I replied with a grin.

"I bet. But there's some truth to it. And here's some advice: move on."

I furrowed my brow and shook my head. "Move on?"

"You lost. Or rather, *we* lost. Because this is not on you. It's on the knuckleheads who allowed it to spin out of 4th-Amendment control. Sure, you got a bum jury verdict, but keep your eye on the ball for the next case and vow to keep fighting, to do better. For the sake of justice. Because given the depravity of humanity, there will be next cases."

"And given the entrepreneurial endeavors of O'Donnell and Associates."

He laughed again and threw back another swig. "Here, here!"

I took a breath and returned my gaze to those glasses resting all peaceful like across the way, considering what he said. Then one end of my mouth curled upward, and I held up my glass with the last swig of scotch.

"To justice, then."

Dean smiled and did the same. "To next time."

We clinked glasses and threw it back.

Indeed. To next time.

Where I'll kick Gideon O'Donnell's bottom from here to Sunday, he won't know what hit him.

All for justice, of course...

STORY 5

NO REST FOR THE WEARY

IT ALL STARTED WITH A SHOE.

A tennis shoe, actually. Or, as my East Coast-bred Ma called them, *sneakers*.

Brand: Adidas. Color: Black. Size: 13.

Kids.

Yep, that's right. Not one of those adult-size pedal coverings. But the smaller variety, for a six- or seven-year-old.

Not brand new one, either. Something worn for months, covered in dirt, smelling sharp and peppery, gum still wedged in the tread. So used, worn.

And belonging to a kid.

Caught sight of it pulling onto Main Street from the state highway zipping all the way from Detroit out our way, following the train tracks that rambled past Mill Creek Junction—and that's when I caught sight of it. Just lying in the gutter under a massive oak, boughs stretching across Main, weighed down by leaves and time. Drove right past at first glance, itching to get back to the farm to close the twelve-hour shift I started from just before normal people eat breakfast, but then I thought better of it.

Was focused on that kickin' Max's Place burger that Burt makes special for me—that thick, juicy patty served rare with an extra amount of moo, still bloody yet warm enough to ward off the salmonella, dripping with sharp Wisconsin white cheddar and smothered in catchup and brown mustard and that special spicy sauce Burt whips up for me when I ask that makes my eyes run. A side of hot fries soaked in grease and sprinkled with a dash of pepper and a generous amount of salt to burn the lips—crack fries, he calls them. All of it complemented by a nice cold bottle of Bud on the side to wash it all down after a long day keeping the Junction safe and sound.

But something in the back of my lizard brain—you know, that deep-seated part of our collective conscious-ness from umpteen years past, nature hammering and honing our biology in such a way that something lodged in the back from ancestors past being chased by mastodons and woolly mammoths just jumps right out atcha.

Well, that black Adidas was that.

Size 13. Kids.

So I reared the pony back on squeaky brakes, then threw her in *Reverse*, easing the Ford Police Interceptor back to the aging, sagging oak.

And there it was.

"What the Sam Hill is that, Roller?" I muttered to myself, running a hand across my magic eight-ball head while the other grabbed the horn and called in my stop to dispatch.

"Need back up, chief?" Sammy came through the black handset wired to the car.

I scoffed. "For a sneaker, Samantha? Just advising at this point. Stand by."

"Roger that," she said, but with that East Coast lilt that sent my blood tingling with enough delight to remind me to grab a coffee with her some time. New girl, imported from Jersey. So 'Roger that' was 'Roga tha.' Sorta stupid for me to note it, but between that and Samantha with straight straw-berry hair insisting on being called Sammy, and that Jersey-girl vibe she had goin'—boy, I tell ya, made me all twitter-pated just exchanging words on the horn. And it wasn't even spring! Guess August dry spells are just as useful for budding love as April showers.

Irregardless, that shoe was calling my name. Or, rather, regardless. Because Ma clued me into the fact that irregard-less wasn't a word last weekend playing Scrabble. It was *regardless*. So she stole my thunder and won with *Qui*. Didn't matter anyway, because I was short an 'r' and would have lost.

But that's besides the point.

What is the point is that the shoe was calling me name, eying it out the front windshield as I idled at the headwaters of Main Street. Something about it didn't feel right. But I couldn't place it.

Until I did.

Kid's right shoe. About six to seven years of age.

The T-Ball Strangler.

My pulse bolted forward like a bucking bronco at the thought. Thought I'd die of a heart attack at the thumpety-thump my ticker threw up. I reached for my glove compart-ment and threw her open, snatching up a packet of sunflower seeds. Tore open the pack and started popping the salted goodness, one by one and then a handful, using the crunch of my favorite snack to ease my mind off the gas pedal from the memory of the only unsolved crime I had to my record.

No way. Can't be...

But what if it was? The serial child killer from a decade ago? The one that nearly sent me to an early grave myself out of sheer exhaustion, compounded by the anger and humiliation at letting the bastard slip through my fingers.

And yet—

A knock at my door interrupted my quiet contemplation, sending my ticker through the roof and a handful of seeds overboard into my lap, my arm jolting at the knucklehead rapping on my window.

"For Pete's sake!" I complained, as much from the embarrassment at being frightened as the annoyance at losing my favorite snack, not to mention the clean up work before I punched the clock.

I set the sack of remaining seeds in my cup holder and glanced outside. Then frowned.

Gideon O'Donnell. Of course. That twerp who'd tanked more Mill Creek Junction PD cases than I'd care to count.

He was covered in sweat and wearing some jogging getup, face beet red. For a second I thought he was in danger, that he needed help. Then I saw him holding a water bottle and popped down the window.

"Hey, chief," he said.

"Gideon. What can I do you for?"

He took a swig from his water and spit it out into the road. Classy. Real classy.

"You know, I could write you up for littering."

He frowned and brought his wrists together and stuck them through the window. "Arrest me, why don't you."

I chuckled and popped a few seeds in my mouth. "Seriously, what's up? I've got things to do, places to be, people to see."

"Just saw you sitting here, right after you put on the brakes and sped backward in reverse."

"As if I would speed up backward in any other direction?"

Gideon paused with furrowed brow. The sarcasm was lost on him apparently.

"Anyway," he went on, "thought I'd stop and say hello."

"And snoop?" I asked, popping another handful of seeds in my mouth.

He smiled, then nodded toward my lap. "What's that you got there?"

I swallowed my seeds and took a swig of my own water. Dasani. Only way to go with the portable H2o. Took a beat to answer, but figured enlisting a citizen could be useful.

"Something that caught my eye," I said, holding the shoe toward Gideon.

He leaned in toward the window, a bit of his runner's BO wafting inside. "That the reason you stopped?"

"That's right." I nodded toward the gutter underneath the oak and added: "Over there, just lying in the road."

He stiffened, looking off toward the side of the road. "In front of John and Jeannie Morgan's house?"

"Uhh..." I squinted in his direction, the red-brick joint coming into view, roof a bit too mossy and sporting that robin's egg-blue door that clashed with the brickwork. "I guess so."

"Black Adidas?"

"Uhh—"

"Kids, size 13?"

Crap. Was I tied to the hip with O'Donnell now?

"As a matter of fact it—"

"That's my case!" Gideon snatched for the shoe, but I was quicker on the draw.

"Hey, that's evidence!" I said.

"You're damn straight! I've been trying to get your office to take the Morgans seriously since this morning!"

I furrowed my brow and shook my head, my brain not at all computing what the Junction's boy-wonder lawyer was talking about. But a cold dread beginning to worm its way from my brain to my bowels just the same. If there was one thing I hated more than anything in the world, it was being caught flatfooted on my turf. The Mill Creek Junction Police Department. If something has been afoot this past day and I didn't know about it—especially when a kid was involved and double especially when Gideon O'Donnell was involved. And given the Morgans were a middle-class black family at the edge of town, with all that's been going on lately in the country...

Crap twice over. No, make that three-times over!

"Slow down, would ya, O'Donnell? Here, let's..." I took a breath and put the pony to rest, turning off the ignition then stepping outside to talk this through.

He was pacing now, as if shaken from the turn.

"You're telling me," I said, holding up the black Adidas that had ruined my day—or made my day, depending on how you looked at it, "that this here shoe belongs to some kid you represent?"

"The parents! And—" he leaned in for a closer look, then mumbled "right shoe," before resuming his pacing again.

"What about the parents?"

He stopped, then faced me. He was getting a little too in my face for my liking. "They hired me this afternoon to try and talk some sense into that Barney Fife detective outfit you've got at Junction PD into taking them seriously that their son was missing."

Barney Fife detective...Almost lost my cheese then and there, but held it together. Although, if what he was saying was true, then under the circumstances I could empathize with the guy—and the Morgans.

Before proceeding, I held up a finger. Then I grasped the shoe at the sole by two fingers and set it on the roof. Reaching back inside the cab to my cruiser, I pulled out a plastic evidence bag. As I stuffed the shoe inside, I cursed myself for not doing it earlier. But how the heck would I know some discarded black Adidas tennis shoe would turn into a missing person's case?

Setting it back on top of the cruiser, I took a breath and said, "Why don't you take it from the top."

Gideon took a breath, then took it from the top. "It's like I said, this afternoon, John and Jeannie Morgan dropped by my office desperate for my help. Their son had gone out to play just after breakfast, but didn't come back when Jeannie went hollering after him."

"Kids do that, don't they?"

"Not Jamal. The kid is like a sheep dog, roaming inside the property lines but not straying."

"What time was this?"

"I already told Detective Bright all this—"

"Well, humor me and tell it again, would ya?" I said, trying not to get irritated but feeling a bit hot under the collar. Not at O'Donnell, but at my own incompetent soldiers for letting this thing drag through the day when a potential missing kid was involved.

He took a swig from his water bottle, then continued, "Around ten. Kid was spraying the hose for an hour."

"Spraying the hose?" I asked.

Gideon shrugged. "It's what kids do. Jamal, at least. Anyway, he was out spraying the lawn, spraying the bushes, spraying the driveway. Next thing Jeannie knows, the hose is lying at the middle of their drive and no sign of Jamal."

A sinking feeling overcame me, that shoe calling for me from the rooftop to find its owner, like it's possessed or something.

"Then what?" I asked, trying to change the subject from the voices rising inside my head from that darn shoe perched on my cruiser rooftop.

"Then, Jeannie went up and down Main Street, looking for the kid. Thought he might be at Old Man Nugent's shop. Jamal loved the guy and loved getting his head buzzed in the summer."

"And nothing?"

He shook his head. "Then she stopped in at Max's, thinking he popped in on his favorite bartender, but he said he hadn't seen the little guy all day. And on she went, from Max's to Millie's on Main to Starbucks—all with the same story."

"Nothing?" I asked, concern rising.

"Nothing."

"And you told Barry all this down at the station?"

"Jeannie and John both did. She'd called up her husband when Jamal went missing to help look for him. Poor couple went to every shop and office and restaurant joint holding up their phones, desperate for some scrap of evidence that their seven-year-old had just been wandering up through the Junction."

"And nothing."

Gideon frowned. "No. And, yeah, Barry Bright took all this down but said his hands were tied since it hadn't been twenty-four hours since the kid was missing. That's when they stormed through my door and hired me to get some answers. I got about as far as them two with the knuckle-head. Said procedure was procedure, and that was that."

I clenched my jaw, my molars grinding against one another and nostrils flaring a bit until I caught myself. Now, I'm a rules kind of guy. Sorta have to be in my gig as chief of police. But there's one thing that I can't tolerate, and that's guys with the policies and procedures manual up their asses when a kid is involved!

I chuckled and shook my head. "Procedure was procedure, huh?"

Gideon nodded. "That's right."

"Well, not if I have anything to say about it." I snatched the shoe from the top off my pony and threw open the driver's side door. "Get in, O'Donnell. We've got a crime to solve."

He hustled around the front and settled inside. Then I gunned it for HQ, Barry Bright in my sights and a missing shoe to get back to its missing owner.

So much for that rare burger still mooin' at me, smothered in Burt's special sauce with a side of sassy fries and that Bud...

No rest for the weary when their is bad still left in the world.

Reminded me of Jesus, actually.

Yes, that Jesus. Not that I'm the regular church-going type or anything, but I memorized my fair share of Scripture. In fact, I showed up to Mill Creek Baptist a few months ago to give that new preacher kid, Peter Daniel Young, for a spin. The guy mentioned how Jesus and his friends had tried to leave the crowds, but they wouldn't let him. Didn't even have them a chance to eat, there were so many people coming and going. As the Bible said, Gospel of

Mark, I believe: *'they went away by themselves in a boat to a solitary place. But many who saw them leaving recognized them and ran on foot from all the towns and got there ahead of them. When Jesus landed he had compassion on them, because they were like sheep without a shepherd. So he began teaching them many things.'*

The man probably just wanted to kick back with a cold one and call it a day, but he sat down and did his thing. Now that's dedication!

No rest for the weary, is right. Not for the Savior of the world; not for Chief Roller, either. That's the sort of relationship I had with my town.

Especially when a kid is involved, with echoes of an unsolved serial killer from a decade ago.

So I brought the strobes of red and blue to life, then tore down Main Street back to HQ, seeking answers and a head named Barry Bright. Who definitely did not live up to his name.

Didn't take long. Soon we were bringing the pony up to the station, and O'Donnell and I were walking inside. I frowned, my stomach echoing the same grumble.

Normally, HQ smelled of damp wood, bleach, and floor wax, with a side of coffee. After all, it is a police department, and an old one at that, standing the test of time for nearly a century. Instead, the place was filled with what smelled like Mickey D's, those Big Macs and Double Quarter Pounders with melty cheese catchup and their special sause, boxes of fries and even those boxed cherry pie thingies.

Not a happy camper.

I ran a clammy hand across my eight-ball head, feeling my blood sugar getting low and stomach eating out my insides. Walking into the bullpen, the whole place was jammed with bodies and bags emblazoned with the Golden Arches.

In the center of it all was Barry Bright, about a donut truck overweight with a receding hairline that put my shiny bald head to shame, his oversized jacket missing but a catchup stain complementing his watered-down mustard-colored dress shirt.

"Chief!" he exclaimed, eyes wide and frantic and indicating trouble. He pushed past a pair of rookies stuffing their faces with fries and looking over a briefing of some sort.

"Where's the fire?" I asked. "And where's my share of the takeout?"

"Uhh...somewhere," the man mumbled, eyeing the room but not looking at anything in particular, clearly rattled and frazzled—which were never a good combo in my line of work.

So I grabbed him by the shoulders and held him stiff. "Bright! What's wrong?"

"We've got a missing person's case. A...uhh...kid!"

O'Donnell and I looked at one another and frowned. "No crap, dingbat!" I said, waving an exclamatory hand in the air while wanting to slap the bozo upside the head.

"Glad you're taking me seriously now!" Gideon said, his face getting red and a vein popping at his temple. Looked like he was about to slug the guy, he was so mad.

Barry just stood there a beat, as if he didn't recognize the guy. Then his mouth dropped and his face went whiter than my bedsheets.

"The M-M-Morgans..." he said with a stutter, the poor guys Achilles heel rearing up under pressure. Then again: "The M-M-Morgans." A little louder this time, as if some loose screw had just slid into place. "The M-M-Morgans!"

he exclaimed, now spinning back toward the bullpen before I spun him back for an explanation.

"What the hell are you babbling about, Barry?"

"Not kid...K-K-Kids!"

I shook my head, not getting it at first.

O'Donnell grabbed my arm. A little close for comfort, and a little too dramatic for the guy. What he said next clarified it all: "Who else, Bright?"

Barry swallowed. "The Hoekstra's son. Thomas."

Now my hunger turned into a topsy-turvy slump at the name. "You're telling me city councilman Hoekstra's son is missing?"

O'Donnell glanced around the bullpen, his face quickly resuming that shade of crimson I thought would lead to blows.

"Is that why you've pulled all these men together?" he said through gritted teeth. "Feeding them and briefing them and getting them all prepped to find Councilman Hoekstra's son? *When you couldn't be bothered to lift a pinky to help a poor, middle-class, BLACK family at the edge of the Junction?!*"

"I-I-I..." Barry stumbled, swallowing before adding: "I didn't know."

"What the hell do you mean you didn't know! Jamal's parents came to you and said their son was missing, for goodness sake!"

"A kid like that disappears from time to time! What did you expect me to do?"

O'Donnell went to reply when his eyes went large, and face went red, and he heaved a breath.

"A kid like tha—"

It happened before I knew what happened, though I should have seen it coming a mile away.

O'Donnell lunged for Barry, the two falling into a desk and sending an extra-large pop spilling across a desk piled high with papers. Someone complained loudly but was drowned out by shouts of alarm at the assault and Gideon swinging at my lead detective.

Managed only one nicely planted right hook across the poor guy's kisser before I managed to wrench O'Donnell off the guy. Truth be told, didn't have much sympathy for the detective, given how he bungled the Morgan's missing person's case, crapping the bed and leaving me as chief to clean up the mess.

"That's assault!" Barry protested, holding a hand to the side of his face.

"A *black* kid that disappears from time to time, you mean? Instead of the upstanding *councilman's* white son?"

Barry looked every bit of the sheep he was, and a wounded one at that. Even I was feeling uncomfortable, my stomach turning over at the optics of it all—especially with everything going on in the world.

I put out a hand to the man and guided him away from O'Donnell.

"You all saw it!" Barry said as we left.

"Let's call it a difference of opinion, shall we?" I said. "Besides, we've got bigger fish to fry, like tracking down two missing Junction kids! One of which is a city councilman's son. And the other just doesn't look good that you gave the parents the brush-off. Have to admit that."

Barry clenched his jaw and nodded, wincing as he took his hand away and glancing back toward O'Donnell.

"Don't worry about him. Worry about the two missing kids. Now, take it from the top. What's the deal with Hoek-stra's boy?"

The man started mumbling a string of details that went

together like one run-on sentence. I told the guy to slow down and just tell it to me straight.

"Which son again?" I asked.

"Their youngest. Thomas."

"How old?"

"Seven."

A shot of adrenaline pinged my gut. Same age as the Morgan's son, the owner of that shoe I'd found.

"When did they notice he was missing?"

"Just after breakfast. Around nine thirty, I think."

My eyes bugged out, and I actually stuck out my neck to emphasize my surprise. "Just after breakfast?"

"That's right."

I took a breath and leaned in, whispering: "That's when the Morgan kid went missing."

Barry glanced at O'Donnell, then back at me.

"Two seven-year-olds go missing, just after breakfast. Both missing their shoes."

Eyes nearly fell out of my sockets on that one. "Your missing kid was missing his shoe?"

"Left one."

"Left?"

He nodded.

"So our two missing kids are missing complementary pairs of shoes?"

Another nod.

"What kind?"

He furrowed his brow and bowed his head, searching for the details. He came up for air and said, "Black Adidas, I think."

"Black Adidas?" I exclaimed. "Size 13?"

"Sounds about right. Why?"

I spread a hand across my now perspiring bald head.

This was getting nuts! And I was dog tired, hungrier than a hyena, and mad as heck I was still on the job.

But, as they say, no rest for the weary.

"Hey, O'Donnell," I called out, motioning for the man to come over. He did. "Check this out." I had Barry relay the details of his case, a truce seeming to have settled between the two.

"So same brand and color, same size but different sides of the pair?"

"That's right," I grunted, all of it feeling real strange.

"And disappearing around the same time?"

"Yep."

Looking to Barry, O'Donnell asked, "Any more kids reported missing today?"

"Not that I'm aware."

Now I looked to Barry. "Not that you're *aware*?"

He clenched his jaw again, his comb-over seeming to rise on an updraft of steamy anger. "No. I'm not. Because nothing else has been reported."

"And neither kid has returned home yet?" I asked. Barry shook his head; O'Donnell frowned and did the same. "I wonder..."

"Wonder what?" O'Donnell asked.

"It's just...what if this isn't what we think it is."

"Isn't what we think what is?" Barry asked, leaning in and folding his arms with skepticism.

I was skeptical myself, but we had to look at it from all angles...

"Do either of you know if the kids are friends?"

"Friends?" O'Donnell asked.

"Yeah. Buddies, pales, amigos? I mean, same age, disappearing around the same time. Summer's almost over with and school will be starting soon. I don't know, maybe they just played hooky from home for the day."

Now O'Donnell crossed his arms, but leaned back instead, as if considering the theory. "Then why the missing shoes?"

Good question.

I shrugged. "Who knows. But what's been done to find the kids so far, other than assembling the largest Mickey D's party this side of the Grand River?"

We both looked to Barry, who stumbled for words. "We were getting to it," he finally offered before bowing his head and mumbling something to himself.

Now my head was about to explore, steam coming up without a comb-over to fluster.

"Get every one of these officers on the street looking for these two kids, Barry. Door to door, if you have it. Shouldn't be too hard to spot. One black kid, one white kid, palling around just before sunset." Then I spun around to leave, adding: "O'Donnell, you're with me."

Maybe it was my stomach talking, nearly chewing through my ribcage now; maybe it was my tired dogs barking for a rest after a long day of law enforcement. Or maybe it was just the old adage that if you want something done right, you've got to do it yourself. Either way, I wasn't waiting around to find these kids.

"What's the plan, chief?" O'Donnell asked once we got back outside the station.

"The plan is to find the kiddos and send their asses into lock up."

"Really?"

Reaching my Crown Vic look-alike, I unlocked the doors and said, "Not the lockup part. But if they've been palling around all day like I suspect, then they might want lockup with what their parents are gonna do to them!"

We got inside and I brought the pony to life.

"You really think they're alright?" O'Donnell asked. "That they've been hanging out this whole time?"

"Only one way to find out."

I peeled back out onto Main Street, and the two of us started driving up and down the thing, looking for the pair who'd messed up my night.

Up and down we drove, seeing nothing but cars and shops closing for the day and revelers coming out to play. We swung by both parks at both ends of town, getting bupkis. Then we revisited their neighborhoods, Jamal's on the outside of town and Thomas's just off of Main, in a leafy well-to-do part of town. Still nothing on the home front.

Checking in with Barry, I'd gotten the same: a big, fat nothingburger. So I swung by the elementary school, taking a stab in the dark at the playground.

And that's when I heard it. Laughter.

Kids, around seven years.

The kind who'd wear black Adidas shoes. And two looked barefoot.

Turning off my lights, I pulled in toward the sound. And there they were, Thomas and Jamal, walking along the edge back toward our position holding ice cream cones and laughing it up, but with another kid around their age, another white kid. And on closer inspection, wearing a pair of black Adidas tennis shoes.

Size 13, if I were to guess. Kid looked a bit younger than the other two but given he was walking between them, laughing it up along with the others, I figured they were all three best buds.

And in deep doo-doo.

They hadn't spotted me, but they were walking toward our position.

I chuckled. "Check this out O'Donnell."

I put on the strobes now and blared the siren. The kids jumped out of their skins from here to next school year!

Good. Served 'em right for giving us all the scare like that.

They looked like they were about to bolt, so I turned off the siren and lights and rolled down my window.

"Thomas, Jamal!" I shouted. They stood statue-still. Good. Right how I wanted 'em. "You ain't in any trouble—" yet, I muttered under my breath, "—but I know some parents who've been worried sick about their kids, and I'd sure love it if we could put their minds at ease and take you home."

They looked at each other, the other kid caught in the middle with eyes as big as saucers. Then they hung their heads, their cones dipping a little, as if they'd resigned themselves to the fact that they had been caught. The trio sauntered over to us as we got out of our cars.

As they came closer, I started counting backwards from five. Needed to center myself before getting the lowdown from the kiddos. Otherwise, I was liable to open a can of it on the youngsters.

I said to the boys, "You do know your parents have been worried sick about you two the whole day, right?"

They looked at each other, taking licks of their melting ice cream and growing silent.

"We thought you were nabbed by some kiddie serial killer."

That did it.

Their eyes snapped open, and they held their heads now.

"So what happened? Where have you been all day?"

"Just around, Chief Roller," Thomas said.

"Around?"

"Yeah, the Junction."

"You know, hanging, chief," Jamal added.

"So you're not hurt," O'Donnell said, stepping into the ring. "Nothing happened to you? No one tried to kidnap you?"

The kids giggled at that. I wanted to join them, because it was more than clear there was nothing more to these rugrats than oblivious kids who gave their parents quite the fright.

But one mystery remained.

I asked, "Why the missing shoes?"

"What missing shoes?" Thomas said.

"The right and left pair of black Adidas shoes."

"Size 13," O'Donnell added.

I sort of knew the answer by then, but wanted to hear it from the kiddos at that point.

"It was for me, Mr. Roller," the other kid said.

I looked at him and said, "What's your name, son?"

"Henry."

"And what was for you?"

He frowned and looked to the other two kids, then said, "I needed some shoes so they each gave me one of their own."

"Then Thomas gave me his other one," Jamal added. "To complete my pair."

"But why?" O'Donnell asked.

The boy shrugged. "Because Henry needed some shoes."

"And that's what friends are for," Thomas said. "When a friend needs shoes, you give him one of your own."

One end of my mouth curled upward. Couldn't help it. Wiser words were never spoken.

But I also had a job to do. And it was getting late; way past my shift and way past their bedtime.

I motioned toward the pony. "Come on, kids, hop in. Let's get you home to your parents."

Which we did, one by one. Parents were sure thankful to get their kids back. Not sure if the kids were all that thrilled, given the story we told their Ma and Pa; definitely wished I'd taken 'em to lockup, given the tongue lashings they were getting. I was just thankful for the happily ever after ending. Especially since the last time something like this happened, where kids had gone missing, things had taken a very different turn.

I offered O'Donnell a ride home, which he gladly took. Pulling up to his two-story brick piece of work, he extended his hand.

"Hey, chief," Gideon said. "Good work."

I offered a tired smile and nodded, then shook it. "You too."

I drove off. Almost went back home to get some shut eye before it all started up again, but that burger and Bud from Max's Place was calling my name. So I answered.

By the time I arrived, the place was half full, some '80s something or other jivin' on the speakers after the last act went to bed. It was seat-your-self service, so I helped myself to the bar.

I hoisted myself onto the stool and slumped down against the polished wood, dog tired yet lighter than the beginning of the end to the day began, that's for sure.

"Your usual, boss?" Max said, slapping down a coaster and setting down a bottle of Bud.

Suddenly, my stomach rumbled with delight, that thick,

juicy patty served rare, dripping with sharp Wisconsin white cheddar and smothered in catchup and brown mustard and Burt's special spicy sauce, a side of those crack fries soaked in grease—all of it sounded oh-so good after a long day keeping the Junction safe and sound.

I took a swig and nodded, keeping at the bottle while Max got the chow started in the back. Man, the American-style pale lager never tasted so good!

Waiting, I watched the tail-end of a baseball game on the flat screen mounted at the back. Couldn't even tell who was playing. Didn't care, either. Needed something to take the mind off the day and unwind.

And what a day it had been. A day that ended with a shoe, of all things. A tennis shoe, a sneaker.

Brand: Adidas. Color: Black. Size: 13.

Kids.

Leading to one thing which led to a whole other thing I was grateful to God in heaven for, considering that alternative.

The T-Ball Strangler.

A jolt of fear, compounded by regret and shame, ricocheted up my spine. Sending me straight back to the Bud, where I finished it and tapped it on the wood bar top as Max walked back over. He popped the top to another and put it in my ready palm.

"So, did you hold back the tide, chief? Keep the peace, fight for justice?"

I smiled, picking at the corner of the red-and-white label wrapped around my beer, knowing what he meant.

The tide of scum and social sickness, wickedness and sheer evil that still plagues our godforsaken world, even a place like Mill Creek Junction, with all its Mayberry facade and small-town charm.

But I loved every minute of it. Because I loved my town. Had a relationship with it, even. Which sounds creepier than it really is. When you're in my line of work, you're married to the town you serve and protect.

Because the job itself is about relationships, all the way down.

Like reconnecting missing kids with their freaked-out parents.

"For another day, partner," I simply said. "For another day."

Max rapped the bar top with his knuckles and nodded. "No rest for the weary, I guess."

I tipped the neck of my bottle toward the man with acknowledgment and took a long swig, then another.

Indeed...

EXPLORE MORE OF MILL CREEK JUNCTION

Welcome to a new story world inspired by such fictional towns as John Grisham's Clanton, Mississippi, and Stephen King's Castle Rock, Maine.

Get to know this world one character, one setting, one event and situation at a time. You're sure to find some of your own story in theirs, while being entertained and inspired for the journey.

Visit www.millcreekjunction.com for more details about the world and a list of short and long-form fiction, following the lives of real people living life and exploring faith.

GET YOUR FREE THRILLER

Building a relationship with my readers is one of my all-time favorite joys of writing! Once in a while I like to send out a newsletter with giveaways, free stories, pre-release content, updates on new books, and other bits on my stories.

Join my insider's group for updates, giveaways, and your free novel—a full-length action-adventure story in my *Order of Thaddeus* thriller series. Just tell me where to send it.

Follow this link to subscribe:
www.jabouma.com/free

ALSO BY J. A. BOUMA

Nobody should have to read bad religious fiction—whether it's cheesy plots with pat answers or misrepresentations of the Christian faith and the Bible. So J. A. Bouma tells compelling, propulsive stories that thrill as much as inspire, offering a dose of insight along the way.

Order of Thaddeus **Action-Adventure Thriller Series**

Ichthus Chronicles **Sci-Fi Apocalyptic Series**

Apostasy Rising / Season 1, Episode 1

Apostasy Rising / Season 1, Episode 2

Apostasy Rising / Season 1, Episode 3

Apostasy Rising / Season 1, Episode 4

Apostasy Rising / Full Season 1 (Episodes 1 to 4)

Apocalypse Rising / Season 2, Episode 1

Apocalypse Rising / Season 2, Episode 2

Apocalypse Rising / Season 2, Episode 3

Apocalypse Rising / Season 2, Episode 4

Apocalypse Rising / Full Season 2 (Episodes 1 to 4)

Faith Reimagined **Spiritual Coming-of-Age Series**

A Reimagined Faith • Book 1

A Rediscovered Faith • Book 2

Mill Creek Junction **Short Story Series**

The New Normal • Collection 1

My Name's Johnny Pope • Collection 2

Joy to the Junction! • Collection 3

The Ties that Bind • Collection 4

A Matter of Justice • Collection 5

Get all the latest short stories at: www.millcreekjunction.com

Find all of my latest book releases at: www.jabouma.com

ABOUT THE AUTHOR

J. A. Bouma believes nobody should have to read bad religious fiction—whether it's cheesy plots with pat answers or misrepresentations of the Christian faith and the Bible. So he wants to do something about it by telling compelling, propulsive stories that thrill as much as inspire, while offering a dose of insight along the way.

As a former congressional staffer and pastor, and award-nominated bestselling author of over forty religious fiction and nonfiction books, he blends a love for ideas and adventure, exploration and discovery, thrill and thought. With graduate degrees in Christian thought and the Bible, and armed with a voracious appetite for most mainstream genres, he tells stories you'll read with abandon and recommend with pride—exploring the tension of faith and doubt, spirituality and culture, belief and practice, and the gritty drama that is our collective pilgrim story.

When not putting fingers to keyboard, he loves vintage jazz vinyl, a glass of Malbec, and an epic read—preferably together. He lives in Grand Rapids with his wife, two kiddos, and rambunctious boxer-pug-terrier.

www.jabouma.com • jeremy@jabouma.com

 facebook.com/jaboumabooks

twitter.com/bouma

amazon.com/author/jabouma